The Accidental Florist

Also by Jill Churchill

JILL CHURCHILL

The Accidental Florist

A Jane Jeffry Mystery

WM
WILLIAM MORROW
An Imprint of HarperCollins*Publishers*

Chu

Jill Churchill can be reached at www.cozybooks.com.

This book is a work of fiction. The characters, incidents, and dialogue are drawn from the author's imagination and are not to be construed as real. Any resemblance to actual events or persons, living or dead, is entirely coincidental.

FIRST EDITION

Designed by Kara Strubel

Title page illustration by John Kane

Library of Congress Cataloging-in-Publication Data

Churchill, Jill 1943–
    The accidental florist: a Jane Jeffry mystery / Jill Churchill. — 1st ed.
        p. cm.
    ISBN: 978-0-06-052845-4
    ISBN-10: 0-06-052845-1
    1. Jeffry, Jane (Fictitious character)—Fiction. 2. Women detectives—Illinois—Chicago—Fiction. 3. Weddings—Fiction. 4. Chicago (Ill.)—Fiction I. Title.

PS3553.H85A65 2007
813'.54—dc22   2006051656

07 08 09 10 11 ❖/RRD 10 9 8 7 6 5 4 3 2 1

The Accidental Florist

Chapter

ONE

J ane pulled into her driveway. She'd just driven to Kansas City and back to drop off Katie at a culinary school at a junior college and get her set up in an apartment with two other girls. Jane had made a quick stop at a liquor store to buy a bottle of champagne on the way home.

She was mixing it with orange juice from the fridge when Shelley knocked at her kitchen door. As Jane opened the door, she said, "You carry the pitcher and I'll bring the glasses. We can sit out on the patio and catch up."

They settled in with Jane's favorite champagne flutes and Jane said, "The trip was easy and rather pretty. So much is blooming along the highways in late May."

"You didn't get lost?"

"Of course we got lost. Several times. But Katie's

turned out to be a pretty good map reader. I got her settled into a little apartment close to the junior college. She has two very nice roommates who are taking the same classes and it's within walking distance."

"She'll do well, I know. Is she still hoping to use the experience to apply to the CIA?"

"Don't call it that!" Jane said with a shudder. "It's the Culinary Institute of America in New York up the Hudson River from the city. And yes, she is. She felt that with the experience of taking summer classes, she'd be better qualified to apply there."

"But she'll miss her senior prom from high school," Shelley said with a laugh.

"She will. It will save me from having to attend another dreadful prom night."

"You've raised good kids," Shelley said, pouring herself a second glass of mimosa.

"So have you, Shelley. Denise is going to go far and so is John. They're both good students and ambitious."

"Ambitious to get out of the house, you mean?"

"Aren't you anxious for that, too?"

"Sort of. But I have longer to wait than you do. My John is a year younger than your Todd. And what is Todd doing this summer?"

"He's looking into colleges on the Internet. He'll only be a junior this fall, but wants to go somewhere where they teach higher mathematics. He's also moved his bed and desk into Mike's room because it faces the street and has better light. He's still working on breaking the code on prime numbers."

"Prime numbers? I've heard of that. But what are they?" Shelley asked.

"The ones that aren't divisible by anything. One, five, seven, eleven, thirteen, seventeen, nineteen, twenty-three, and so forth. He has a fancy grid program and put in numbers up to twenty thousand; he left all the ones that can be divided by two in black, and highlighted the ones in red that can't be divided by three, five, seven, and so on."

"So what's his conclusion?"

Jane sighed. "He doesn't have one yet. But the higher the numbers the less frequent they are. He's trying them out on all sorts of different grids to see if he can find a pattern. So far he hasn't."

"He's a dogged kid, isn't he? I remember when he was obsessed with building the biggest thing possible with Legos."

"But, Shelley, that cost me the earth and created huge storage problems. This costs me nothing and if he ever finds out the secret to prime numbers, he'll become rich and famous," Jane said with her fingers crossed and wearing a big grin.

"So Katie's gone, Todd's obsessed, and Mike's in graduate school in Indiana for the summer. It must be a lot quieter at your house. I envy you."

"Thank you. I can't remember you ever saying that," Jane said, still smiling. "I'm also a better driver than you, but you'd never admit that."

"You're just a slower driver," Shelley said, watching Jane's two now-elderly cats, Max and Meow, heading for the field behind their two houses. "Do they ever catch anything back there anymore?"

"Not anymore. And you notice they clawed their way over the fence instead of bounding over it like jackrabbits the way they used to."

Shelley laughed. "Wouldn't we both do that if we were as old as they are in cat years?"

Jane had just taken a sip of her drink and had almost snorted it out her nose. "I hope we'd have a little more dignity than the cats though," she said when she quit coughing.

Jane poured herself a second mimosa. The goblets were tall but narrow and one wasn't enough. Besides, the pitcher would lose its bubbles if any were left over.

"We have to finish this pitcher," Jane said. "It won't keep fuzzy and tickle our noses."

"Might as well. Neither of us are going anywhere tonight, are we?"

By dusk, when the cats climbed back over the fence, Meow limping a little, both Jane and Shelley were tiddly. Jane stood up to call the cats in and almost lost her balance.

"Jane, you're drunk."

"No, I'm not. I drove all day long and then sat out in the setting sun drinking diluted champagne. That's all. Let's see how you find your own way home."

"I just live next door, Jane," Shelley said, standing and waving her arm, nearly tumbling over her chair.

"Coffee," Shelley pleaded. "Strong coffee. I'm not sure I can get home without crawling across both our driveways."

Holding on to each other, with the cats wreathing around their ankles, they made their way to Jane's kitchen. "I have to feed the cats first or they won't leave us alone."

Jane spilled a third of the cat food on the floor. She looked down and giggled. "They'll eat it anyway."

Shelley had also spilled some of the coffee mix on the counter. They sat down at the kitchen table, listening to the cats crunching their food and smelling the coffee brewing. Every now and then, one or the other of them laughed softly at nothing.

"Can you pour the coffee or should I?" Jane asked.

"First one who can stagger across the room will."

Shelley won because Jane skidded on some of the hard little cat food pellets. They made their way carefully to the living room, carrying the cups that were only half full so they wouldn't spill, and sipping while watching Paula Deen cooking a pork roast on the Food Network.

In two minutes, Jane burped slightly and said, "Let's watch something else that's not about food. I'm still a little dizzy and food doesn't sound good."

They watched *Curb Appeal* instead. It was an episode Jane had seen at least twice before, but she didn't care.

Shelley finally got up when the show was finished and said, "I have to go home and take a little nap."

Jane went to her kitchen door to watch her leave. Both

of their cars were in the adjoining driveways. Shelley was walking well, but lightly touching the hoods to make sure of her footing. When she reached her own kitchen door, she made a victory sign to Jane and went inside.

Jane also decided a nap was a good idea in spite of it being only seven in the evening. She went to the stairs to her bedroom and paused for a moment. She could crawl up them safely, but Todd might come out in the hallway and realize she was still a little tipsy. So she clung to the stair rail and called out to Todd when she got to the top landing, "I'm just back from a long drive and I need a short nap."

There was no reply. The door to his room—Mike's old room—was closed.

Jane didn't wake until morning, still in the clothes she'd worn the day before. At least she didn't have a hangover. In fact, a good night of deep sleep had cheered her up considerably. She went to the bathroom to brush her teeth before showering and was horrified at the state of her hair. She looked as if she'd been in close contact with a tornado overnight. A really punk-looking hairdo.

Her first published book about Priscilla was coming out in about two weeks. She'd been surprised at what a slow process publishing was. First her agent had a few minor corrections to suggest. Jane made them. Then the editor had a few more to be made. Then the copy editor went at it hammer and tongs. When all that had been done, there were requests for input on the cover copy and blurbs. And then her editor faxed copies of the cover and placement of her name. By that time nearly a year had passed and Jane had finished the next one, except for letting it sit and stew before rereading the final draft. Good thing they had a picture of her looking a whole lot better than she did this morning.

Chapter

TWO

The next morning, when Jane went out for the newspaper, Shelley was coming inside with hers. They
made no mention of the day before. Shelley looked as
chipper and normal as Jane did now that Jane had fixed
her hair. The cats had indeed eaten all the spilled cat food
and Jane had cleaned up the floor. "I have coffee brewing.
I found a new brand at a Starbucks in Kansas. A hint of
hazelnut flavoring, I think. But not saying so on the container. Want to try it out with me?"

"Sure," Shelley said, pitching her own newspaper on
her kitchen porch. "Isn't it odd that all the houses on this
block were constructed with the kitchen in the front of
the house?"

"I like it that way," Jane said. "I can sit at the kitchen table and see what's going on along the street."

"So do I," Shelley agreed. "This coffee is good. I wonder if our own Starbucks carries it as well?"

"I've always just had their mocha when I buy it there. We'll have to go look and see next time we stop by."

"Are you ever going to marry Mel?" Shelley asked.

Jane gawked at her. "Surprisingly, I've been thinking a lot about it. You know he tried to give me an engagement ring that awful Christmas that his furnace died, and he and his dreadful mother, Addie, stayed here. I said I'd keep it for later. But he decided I might lose it and he took it back and put it in his bank lockbox."

"Do you suppose he still has it? After all, you and he have had a very long, happy relationship and now that you're going to have only one child at home most of the time, you should consider it."

"Do I have to propose to him?" Jane asked with a glint in her eye.

"Why not? You're an independent woman. Not a wimp. The worst that could happen is that he'd turn down the offer. And you know he wouldn't."

"I'm fairly sure you're right. I'd like for him to live with me in this house. It would mean giving up several closets and cleaning out the other half of the garage for his precious MG."

"When did you become so practical?" Shelley asked.

"All these years hanging out with you," Jane replied.

"You're the most sensible, practical woman I know. Except for your give-'em-hell driving habits."

"You'll note, I hope, that I've never been in an accident," Shelley claimed.

"But other people you terrified have ended up in ditches, I'd bet."

"I never look back," Shelley said proudly.

Jane was quiet for a few minutes and then said, "I'm going to have to plan my proposal to Mel. I don't think, 'You wanna get married, big guy?' is quite appropriate."

"Ask first if he kept the ring he tried to give you. Would that be a way to start a proposal?"

"Good idea. Thanks."

As it happened, Mel called Jane later in the day and said, "Want to go to your favorite pricey restaurant tonight? I have something to tell you about."

He sounded so serious that Jane was scared. Was he getting ready to dump her just as she was about to propose marriage?

"Of course I'd like that," she said, trying to make it sound as if she meant it.

"You sound wary," Mel said. "It's not a bad thing. Just something I suggest you and Shelley might want to do."

Jane sat down at the kitchen table, thinking that he'd come to understand her a little bit too well. "I can't wait to hear what it is. What time should I be ready?"

"I've already made reservations for seven. Is that okay?"

"It's fine. I'll leave a sandwich and chips for Todd."

"Can't he do that himself?" Mel asked, sounding sincerely confused.

"Sure he could. But I'm a mom."

Mel was quiet but relaxed as they drove to the restaurant. They always had a private booth where they couldn't be overheard. The waiter handed them the poster-sized menus, asked if they wanted a drink while they studied the menu, and disappeared to get each of them a glass of the house merlot.

They both knew what they wanted. Jane chose a green salad and chicken scalloppine. Mel wanted a salad and the largest filet mignon on the menu. They might choose desserts later.

The waiter returned with the restaurant's signature rye bread rolls and butter along with their drinks, took their orders, and disappeared.

"What is it you wanted to tell me about?" Jane asked when she'd finished a roll and tasted her drink.

"It's about your and Shelley's safety."

"I don't understand. Is this police work? Are we in some kind of danger we don't know about?"

"In a way. But it's not a police secret. Women are attacked far more often than men. Men tend to fight back, and I don't think either of you would have the strength to do so. There is this tough old woman who teaches women how to better protect themselves. I thought it would be useful to you and ease my mind about your welfare."

"But Shelley and I don't go bar hopping at night. We know better than that."

"That's not the point. And crimes against women don't always happen at night anyway."

"Is it expensive to take these classes?"

"No, they're almost free. You only pay a couple bucks for the rental of the meeting hall."

"When do they start?"

"Next Monday. Two a week for two weeks. And further lessons in self-defense if it interests you two." He reached into a pocket inside his suit coat and handed her a sheet of paper. "This is all the information. It would really ease my mind if you knew more about protecting yourselves when you're out and about."

"I'll show this to Shelley," Jane said, perusing the items on the list. "It meets during the day, I'm glad to say."

"She does night classes, too. For women who can't get off work in the daytime. I'm glad you're considering this."

"I'm sure it will be interesting to both of us," Jane said. She folded the paper and tucked it into her purse. She'd noticed that the waiter was hovering.

Stuffed to the brim with rolls, salad, and dinner, they strolled out and got into Mel's car. As he approached her house, Jane said, "Could we stop for a few minutes at that little park down the block before you drop me off?"

He glanced at her, wondering why she wanted to do this, but did as she asked. When he turned the ignition off, Jane said, "Do you just happen to have kept that engagement ring you tried to give me long ago?"

Mel grinned. "I did. Do you want it back?"

"Yes. It's time. Past time, in fact."

"It's in my safety-deposit box. I'll bring it over tomorrow. Janey, are you sure you want it?"

She tried to hug him, but it's hard to do in a little MG. "I'm absolutely sure I do."

Mel stepped out of the car, came around, and gave Jane his hand. "Get out of there right now. I want to kiss you without either of us getting hurt trying it in the car."

Jane was very late getting home. She could see from outside that Todd's room was dark. She all but danced up the stairs.

The next morning Mel dropped in on his way to work. He didn't look quite as happy as he should have.

"What's wrong? Has the ring gone missing?" Jane asked.

"No, it's my mother."

"She's missing?" Jane asked.

"I wish she were. I made the mistake of calling her to tell her the good news that we're getting married . . ."

"She didn't take it well, I guess," Jane said, not the least bit surprised.

"It's not exactly that. It's . . ."

"Mel, spit it out and get it over with. She's refusing to come?"

"Far from it," he said. "Let me put the ring on your finger and we'll sit out on your patio and talk about it."

They sat close together and Mel reluctantly explained. "See, I'm her only son."

"I know that."

"But she says your parents have two daughters."

"That's true. So what is the problem with it?" She was looking at the ring on her finger, smiling, and thinking she'd forgotten how beautiful it was. "Your mother also has two daughters. She mentioned them that Christmas she stayed at my house."

"It's this. I'll just hit you with it. And you can smack me upside the head for saying it. My mother will do the rehearsal dinner."

"That's what she's supposed to do."

"She wants to do the whole wedding as well."

Mel bent his head, waiting for her reaction.

Jane laughed like a loon. "Do you think this is a surprise to me? I've met your mother, remember. It's just what I'd expect her to do. Roll over everybody with a tank."

"You're not angry?"

Chapter

THREE

J ane said, "No, I'm not angry. Before I asked you about the ring, I gave a lot of thought to a wedding. Here is how it's going to go. First, it happens when my parents can be there. They're in Denmark right now. Dad's translating for some Americans who want a contract to do something about drainage in Denmark.

"Second, when my parents come, we'll have the real wedding in front of a judge with just family. Shelley, as my matron of honor, my kids, I probably have to invite my mother-in-law, Thelma, and whoever you want as best man.

"Third, Mel, there are things your mother *cannot* do. That Christmas she spent here she asked me what the green and white leaves I had in a bowl were called. I told her they were ivy. She said she had some sort of the same thing on a tree in her yard, but it was bigger, darker, and never got red berries. I had to explain that they didn't get berries. Those were red beads I'd glued on. She wouldn't know a lily from a rose. So that's why I'm going to make the choice of flowers for my bouquet, and the flowers on the dining tables. I'll write all this down so you can tell her about it. And I'll also pay for the flowers and mail her a copy of the rules for her fake wedding. So she can't choose the flowers for the wedding she wants to do. And she can't suggest what I wear."

Mel, looking poleaxed, said, "Could your uncle Jim be my best man? I've always admired him."

"Good. That's who I would have suggested. He thinks the world of both of us.

"So that's settled." She didn't want to get distracted from her main theme. "There is a fourth set of rules. Your mother can foot the bill for the second wedding. She can choose the food. She can choose the wine and invite mobs of her professional friends. She can't add bridesmaids who are the wives, girlfriends, or daughters of her rich clients. Same for groomsmen. She doesn't choose the hotel or church where the wedding will be held."

"She's not going to like this, Janey."

"'Frankly, my dear, I don't give a damn,' to quote Rhett Butler. It's our fake wedding. And the bride and her parents make the decisions. I know they would agree with me since your mother has demanded to run the whole thing. You have to stand up to your mother on this or there's only the one wedding at the judge's chambers."

Mel put his hands over his ears, and suddenly started laughing. "Whatever you say. I wish you could be around when I tell her this. But you can't be. Because she's going to be very nasty about it. Will you do me a favor in return?"

"Probably. What is it?"

"Wear that gorgeous emerald-colored suit Shelley made you buy. You look beautiful in that. And I want your uncle Jim to be best man for both weddings."

"That's doable. You really are my heart's desire." She started to tear up and Mel put his arms around her and kissed her forehead.

Jane's father couldn't get out of his translating duties for the Danes until the end of July, but her mother could come. Jane found this unacceptable. She didn't care when the wedding took place and Mel didn't either. So they'd wait till both of her parents could be there.

In the meantime, Jane started making lists. What closets would need to be purged? At least two.

How many more towels would she need when she was married. "Go for it," she said out loud. "Buy all new ones. Blue for him. Pink for me."

Another thing was getting the other half of the garage cleaned out. She'd gone to look it over and there wasn't a thing in the other half that was worth more than a couple of bucks. Old tablecloths that had mildewed, the lawn mower, a leaf blower, a snow blower, even a lot of the kids' old, dirty, disintegrating toys. If Todd wanted that half a million LEGOs, he'd have to find a different place to store them or give them away to somebody younger.

Meanwhile, she'd go pick out an attractive shed to put at the side of the house to keep all those tools in. She'd go to Sears and make them bring one out and put it together. Then she'd hire some local teenage boys from the neighborhood to move everything into it. In fact, Shelley's son, John, would probably be glad to do it for the right amount of money. She'd ask Shelley about it.

And what about that beat-up desk and disgraceful butt-sprung chair Mel loved to use when he was working at home? Where would that go?

Todd's room? He'd moved his desk and bed into Mike's bedroom. Mike might want it back someday.

What about extending the house at the back behind the dining room? She could afford it. Thanks to her dead ex-husband's will, she had a perpetual third interest in the Jeffry family pharmacy because she'd contributed a substantial sum she'd inherited from a great-grandmother when the single Jeffry Pharmacy was about to file for bankruptcy.

They'd expanded all around Chicago over the years and she'd been able to pay for the kids' colleges as the Jeffrys' business spread. Now there were two more nearly ready to open in a pricey neighborhood in St. Louis and another in Indianapolis. She could afford to make Mel his own office. What a good wedding present that would be!

It couldn't be a surprise, however. He'd want to be

involved. And he could figure where the windows would be, where to put his files, the desk and chair, and the old cowboy lamp he'd had as a boy.

Jane went to Shelley's house as soon as Mel left. She explained about the rules she'd made for Addie's wedding after the real wedding with just her own family and Shelley's.

Shelley said, "I'm so proud of you! You'd thought this all out and were ready. But where does Addie get her money? When she stayed here that Christmas, she was talking to someone about hauling around celebrities. That can't be all that profitable."

"She only did that for two years," Jane explained. "Then she studied to be a Realtor. And stole all the richest people from everyone else. But there's a payoff."

"What payoff?"

Jane told her that Mel had already insisted that the two of them needed to attend four classes in Women's Safety.

"Why? We're careful already. We don't go out cruising bars in the evenings."

Jane explained Mel's reasoning, and Shelley admitted he might have a good point. And it might even be interesting.

While Jane was planning all she had to do before the wedding, she and Shelley went to take their first class in Women's Safety. On the way, Jane said, "I e-mailed my dad that I was going to marry Mel and wanted them here. He e-mailed back, 'Please tell me you're not pregnant.' He has a good sense of humor—he thinks."

The class was held on the ground floor of one of the buildings in a group of middle-class apartment buildings with what appeared to be a little-used community center in the middle of them. There were grocery stores, florists, and drugstores on the ground floors of a lot of them.

Most of the class had already assembled. There were only seven of them at the meeting. The leader called them to attention. She was something of a surprise. She looked to be around fifty years of age, but Mel had referred to her as an old lady.

Jane whispered this fact to Shelley. "We're getting closer to being fifty ourselves."

"Never say that again," Shelley snapped. "She must be older than we think. Lots of plastic surgery until you look at the turkey skin on her throat."

The woman called the class to order. "I'm Miss Elinor Brooker Welbourne. And never call me Ms. Let's get your first names sorted out."

Everyone obeyed in turn. Except the youngest, a girl of about twenty who was dressed in a long-sleeved blouse and jeans in spite of it being a hot afternoon. She said she was Sara Tokay.

"All right. Show me your purses before we begin."

An odd request, Jane thought, but they all obediently complied.

"Jane has the best. But you kept it under your chair. Don't ever do that again."

"Why?" Jane asked boldly.

"Because it's dangerous. Anybody behind you could have hooked it with their foot and gone through it."

This remark resulted in some outraged muttering from two of the other women. "As if we'd steal someone's purse!" one said.

Miss Welbourne ignored this. "Purses are important. Jane's has a long strap. But she should wear it crossed over her opposite shoulder and in front of her. Purse snatchers would be glad to take any of the other purses the rest of you brought with you."

She went on, "I have the names of two cobblers in Chicago who could install a flexible steel wire in the strap, so purse snatchers couldn't cut through it with a sharp knife or box cutter. I'll give you their names and addresses at the end of this session."

"That's interesting," Shelley whispered to Jane.

Miss Welbourne went on to explain about pickpockets. She said, "Always buy trousers, skirts, and jackets with pockets, preferably with button closures, and put your cash and one credit card in one front pocket. Leave the other credit cards behind in a safe place at home. Also put your driver's license in your other front pocket. And never put a house key in your handbag or billfold. If you have a driver's license in your purse, it gives them your home address and the key to your front door." She suggested as well that women who operated on largely a cash basis, only take along with them to the grocery store or a shop what they could afford to lose.

"Leave the rest of your cash at home, well hidden. It would be a good idea to purchase a small, fireproof, waterproof safe and keep it somewhere it's unlikely to be found easily."

Jane was sitting next to Shelley with Sara Tokay on her other side. Sara pushed her sleeve back to look at her wristwatch.

"This is enough for you to absorb in this first meeting. We'll get together and go over some other matters on Thursday morning."

Jane was doing as she'd been told, holding her purse in front of her passing the strap over one shoulder and under and in front of the other arm.

"That was good advice," she said as she hauled herself up into Shelley's minivan. "Did you see that young girl's arm when she looked at her wristwatch?"

"I didn't notice she did that. Why do you ask?" Shelley said, shoving the car into drive and shooting out of the parking lot at a furious rate. Jane, as always, had her foot firmly on the nonexistent brake pedal on the passenger side.

"Because the girl had a terrible bruise on her arm."

"That's a bit alarming. But maybe she was careless and got it herself," Shelley said, taking a sharp right turn that felt as if she'd done it on only the right wheels.

"Maybe. Or maybe not," Jane said.

Chapter

FOUR

The next day, Jane called Shelley to borrow Shelley's son, John.

"Sure. What for?"

"I need to get all the stuff in the other half of my garage either thrown away or put into a shed at the side of the house. I want John and Todd to go with me to Home Depot and Sears to pick one out."

"May I come along?" Shelley asked. "I fancy I'd be good at picking out a shed that looked nice."

"Sure. The more the merrier. I want whoever will put it together for free."

When they were ready to go, and told the boys about the project, both of them said, "Putting a shed together is easy. We can do it for you. Also pick up another trash bin to throw out the junk."

It was, naturally, Shelley who took a measurement of how much width could fit between the fence and the house. "And you need two big doors that open out," she said as they took off at warp speed in her minivan.

Todd and John didn't seem to mind riding with Shelley at the wheel. Jane thought it was because they were too young to contemplate imminent death in a fire-engulfed vehicle. Or simply because they had male genes.

They found a perfect steel shed that met the requirements and could be delivered and stacked in the driveway the next day. In the meantime, Jane went out to buy a new trash bin and started filling it. It would probably take two weeks to get everything disposable in the garage into it.

Jane then turned her attention to making an office for Mel. She hadn't consulted him yet. But she called her honorary uncle Jim. He'd had a room tacked onto the back of his house three years earlier. He was close to retirement and wanted to set up a woodworking room with lots of windows for good light.

"Don't mention this to Mel yet. I want to tell him about it and figure out how much room he needs."

Jim said, "You'll need an architect to draw up tentative plans, and get the township's permission. I can help you with that. I've been through it, and know the ropes and the right people to hire."

"Uncle Jim, you really are a treasure."

"I'm looking forward to the wedding. I haven't seen

Cecily and Michael for two years." Uncle Jim had been a long-term Chicago cop. Before that he served as a bodyguard for five years when Jane's parents traveled to different countries. They'd always been close to him.

"We scheduled the wedding around their timetable."

Jane had already called her son, Mike, to tell him she was getting married. His response was merely, "It's about time, Mom. You're not getting any younger."

Katie was slightly less enthusiastic, but pretended prettily that she was pleased.

Todd had taken the news easily, "Cool, Mom. Somebody else to take out the trash every week."

Thelma took it very badly. "At your age, you're getting married? What's the point in doing something so foolish?"

"That's my business, Thelma. It's not your concern."

Jane went on to explain that the real wedding was going to be in a judge's chamber with just her family and Mel's. "You're welcome to attend if you wish. Mike and Katie and Todd will all be there, as well as my friend Shelley and Uncle Jim."

"I'll have to think about it. Issue me an invitation and directions," Thelma snapped and hung up.

Jane let out a long sigh. Why had she ever even considered inviting Thelma? She should have known she'd be nasty. Just not quite as nasty as she had been.

She'd send the invitation and just hope the old tartar wouldn't show up and be rude to Jane and everyone else.

The next day, four big boxes appeared in her driveway.

She assumed they were the pieces of the shed. If not, she couldn't imagine what else would come in such big boxes. She called Shelley and told her to get the boys ready and asked if she had a box cutter with a fresh blade. She wasn't surprised that Shelley had one handy. The boys were excited. They'd already dug up the grass and leveled the area where it would sit. Todd had found an old painting tarp with pink paint speckles. Whatever was it doing in the garage? Jane wondered. Nothing in the house had ever been painted pink. They'd put it on the ground and set all the bags of screws and handles in the right order.

Jane and Shelley decided to watch the process. They took two patio chairs out on the lawn. The boys moved the table and the umbrella for them, in a bit of a temper because it was slowing them down.

The boys did a good job. They, unlike Jane, read all the directions before starting. Jane never read the instructions until she realized she'd done something wrong.

Late in the afternoon, she called Mel and said, "I'm making chili this evening. I know it's winter food but I have a craving for it. I want to show you my new shed as well."

"A new shed?"

"To clear out the other side of the garage for your car," she explained. "All the big stuff is already in there and most of the rest is going out in the trash."

She didn't mention the pictures she'd found of Mike and Katie going camping as little kids with their father. They grabbed at her heart. He was a good dad. Just not a faithful husband.

Mel looked a bit wrung out when he arrived for dinner. "Your mother?" she asked.

"Yup. I won't even tell you what she said."

"It was probably as bad as what my mother-in-law said to me yesterday. Forget it. I'm sticking to my guns about the rules. No matter how mad your mother is, does she understand that I mean it?"

"She does. But I need to reinforce it several times before the wedding."

After the chili was chowed down, she called for Todd and John to come show off their work. Even Mel was impressed. "Now let's see the garage." He was pleased.

Jane said, "Wait for what will impress you more. Let's sit outside for a while."

When Mel had carried the table, umbrella, and chairs back to the patio, and they'd taken their coffee cups and some store-bought chocolate chip cookies to nibble, Jane sprang her plan on Mel.

"I'm building you an office just behind the dining room."

"Jane, you can't do that. You don't know how, in the first place, and it would be too expensive. You could just clear out that big closet-sized sewing room."

"It's too small. And where would I put my sewing machine?"

"When did you last use it?"

"Oh, I think it was around 1923."

That made Mel laugh again. He hadn't even smiled earlier.

"I've consulted Uncle Jim. He put in a room for his retirement hobbies. He knows who to ask. As for the expense, consider it a long-term wedding gift. You would feel too guilty to ever leave me."

"Jane, quit joking. It would cost the earth."

"Mel, I don't think you realize how much money I have. When I married the first time, my husband was a one-third owner of the family pharmacy. They were about to go under. It was a rental and the owner raised their rent by half again what it had been. I used a fairly large inheritance I'd received to help them get a better location."

"That was good of you," Mel admitted.

"Not really. If the business had gone belly-up my husband would have lost his job. Anyway, he wrote a will in which it said that if he died before I did, he wanted his third of the business profits to go to me for all time. And he did die. Running off to meet his bimbo on an icy night."

"You never told me that part," Mel said. "You just said it was a car accident."

"I don't tell many people. Only my kids and Shelley know. And the kids don't know *why* he was out that night and never will. So the upshot of this long story is that the family pharmacy has spread like a veritable plague. There are Jeffry pharmacies all over the Chicago area, and they're opening two in St. Louis this month and one in Indianapolis. I still get my third share of the profits. And they're substantial. In short, I can afford to build out a new room where you can have lots of space, lots of light, and all your stuff. And if you don't want to use it, I'll do it anyway as a storeroom. By the way, my first book about Priscilla comes to the bookstores in a week or two and I also make a nice little wad of money when it does. I could store my author's copies of my book in that room if you really don't want it," she said with a sly smile.

"Then I'm going to take you up on this. Without feeling like a kept man."

"Too bad. I intend to keep you at least until we're both using walkers and hauling around oxygen canisters on rollers to go to cheap buffet dinners."

Mel laughed out loud. "It's a deal, Janey."

Chapter

FIVE

The architect Uncle Jim had recommended was quick to contact Jane early the next morning.

"Jim and I are old friends. We shared a dorm room back in college. He told me you needed advice on adding a room for your soon-to-be husband. He thinks the world of the man you're marrying. So I'd like to meet with both you and Detective VanDyne as soon as possible. By the way, I'm Jackson Edgeworth." He gave her his office number.

"Anytime is good for me except this morning," Jane said. "A friend and I are attending a class Mel recommended. I'll call him and ask if later today suits him, if that's convenient for you," Jane said, thinking how timely his call was.

She phoned Mel, saying, "The architect my uncle

Jim suggested wants to know if you could be free this afternoon?"

"I'm due some time off. I could just take today off if you want."

"I'll call him back right now and tell him to pick the time and let you know."

When she reached Mr. Edgeworth, she said, "Mel and I are both free anytime today in the afternoon if you wish to choose a time."

"How about one in the afternoon? I have an appointment this morning."

"May I confide in you?" Jane asked.

"I suppose so."

"Whatever amount of space Detective VanDyne suggests, increase it by half. He's worrying that it will be too expensive. And I'm not."

The man chuckled. "Half again as big is nowhere near half again the price. I'll make that clear. Give me your address and I'll get my secretary to check the city codes and setback allowances and all that bothersome stuff before I come over."

Jane reported back to Mel and he agreed to the time. She didn't mention her concerns about the size, but did pass on that Mr. Edgeworth would know all the township rules before he arrived.

The class in Women's Safety was about traveling around. "If you get off the El at the wrong station, and find yourself in a frightening part of town, go to the nearest shop, a deli or such. Be very pleasant to the clerk. They're more likely to be helpful. Find out when the next train comes. Most places carry schedules. Buy something. A bottled drink and a pack of chips, and if you prefer to ask them to call a taxi for you, wait inside at a window for it, not on the street, exposing yourself to criminals."

Miss Welbourne paused for this to sink in and then added, "Make sure you look confident. Don't fret or look as if you're scared. Don't stand around reading a map or a magazine. Keep your eyes out for anyone watching you. If you've called a taxi, walk briskly out of the shop and get in it fast. Same thing if you go back to the El station. Stand on the platform looking brisk and confident. Not worried. Keep your back to a wall so nobody can come up behind you.

"Malls, too, can be dangerous. Especially dress shops," she went on. "If you want to try something on, don't hang your handbag on the hook on the door. Place your bag under a chair as far from the door as you can and throw your own clothing over it to conceal the bag.

"If you're going to a movie or the theater, don't sit at the end of a row. You're more vulnerable there. If you can help it don't sit near anyone who looks suspicious. Keep your handbag on your lap with your hands crossed over it. Don't put it under your seat at all costs. Someone behind you could just hook a foot under the chair and take it."

Most of the class was making notes and Miss Welbourne waited patiently for them to catch up.

Then she went on. "If you go to a bar or restaurant try to get a booth. If it isn't possible, sit where you aren't in a chair that many people have to walk by. Don't sit near an aisle that leads to the bathrooms. There will be a lot of people walking past you. Keep your handbag on your knees and cross your legs while you study the menu and eat. While you're waiting for your food to come, keep your bag in your lap with your hands crossed over it. Don't read a book or magazine while you are waiting for your drink or food. Keep an eye out for anyone who is staring at you and don't make eye contact once you realize it.

"There is another reason you want a booth if you can get one. That's so if you're young and pretty, you should put your drink as far away from people walking by as you possibly can. This date rape drug is getting to be a serious problem and it's so easy for a man to just pass his hand over a glass as he walks by."

"Speaking of young and pretty, where is that cute little Sara girl? She's not here this time," one of the women asked.

Miss Welbourne sighed. "I wasn't going to tell you this, but I feel now that I must. The police alerted me this morning that her boyfriend beat her to death last night."

Everyone exclaimed "Poor girl" or "What a tragedy" or simply, "Oh no."

Miss Welbourne looked as if she'd caved in on herself. "I'm sorry to cut this class short, but I don't believe we can go on more today. At least, I can't. Go home."

She left the room ahead of them, her briefcase in one

hand, and her handbag properly crossing her chest and in front of her.

"That's terrible news," Shelley said on the way home. "She was so young."

"Young or old, it's tragic. It's probably the reason she was taking the class."

"And maybe he found out she was doing so," Shelley commented.

It wasn't until Jane had closed her kitchen door and set her purse on the kitchen table, that it occurred to her that Mel might be in charge of this murder case. And wouldn't get the day off tomorrow after all.

She tried to get him at his office. His secretary told her he was just finishing up in a meeting. He'd call back in ten minutes.

When he did, she told him what Miss Welbourne had said about Sara. "You're not on this case, are you?"

"No. It was inner city. Your uncle Jim has it. Nice case just before he retires."

"Nice?" Jane almost yelped.

"Well, not nice. But good for him. He's virtually solved it. Her blood is all over the boyfriend. All over the lamp he hit her in the head with and on the lamp cord he strangled her with."

Jane sat down at the kitchen chair, stretching the phone cord as far as she could. This conversation made her woozy.

"I just meant that your uncle Jim will get the credit, and a lot of publicity to retire on. Leaving after all the photo flashbulbs as he announces that it's official that the case is solved."

Jane got a grip on herself. "So you'll be here when the architect meets with us?"

"Of course. Not my case. I'm free all day. I'm sorry Miss Welbourne told the class."

"She was asked why the girl wasn't at the meeting this afternoon. She was so upset to say it that she dismissed the class early."

"Speaking of the class, are you learning useful information?"

"Oh yes. She's told us lots of things we should have had the common sense to have realized and hadn't. There are just two more classes. Shelley and I are going to be much more careful of ourselves from now on. I'm glad you forced us to do this."

"I didn't force you. Just suggested."

"Hmmm," was all Jane could say, except for adding, "I'll see you at one then."

Jane was surprised at Edgeworth's appearance. He'd sounded younger than he was. Well, of course. He went to school with her uncle Jim. He was wearing a lightweight tartan jacket, a red shirt, black trousers, and had a full head of thick curly white hair. "Hello, Ms. Jeffry. Your uncle thinks the world of you."

"He's not really my uncle. He's my parents' longtime best friend. And please call me Jane."

"Call me Jack, then. And Detective VanDyne, may I call you by your first name?"

"Sure. I'm Mel."

Jack put his briefcase down and pulled out a fresh legal pad and a yellow pencil. "Let's start with the dining room. That's where we'll cut through. I've checked the code and regulations. You are able to extend the back of the house twenty-two feet."

Jane led him to the dining room. He looked around. "Nice room. Could that china hutch go on the end of the room or next to the window on the other side?"

"Sure. I can't move it myself. But if I empty it out and have help, we could put sliders under it."

"Good. Now let me check the studs."

He used a gadget that he moved across the room at the same height. A little red light showed up from time to time and the device made a feeble little beep. "Just what I'd expected. The right intervals."

He laughed. "In the old days, I'd have tapped it with my knuckles and known from the sound where the studs were, but my son insists that I use this gadget. Do either of you care which end of the room you want the entrance door?"

Jane and Mel looked at each other and shrugged.

"I never thought about it. In the middle?"

Jack shook his head. "That would break the look of this wall. I'd suggest the far wall. But still move that furniture so Mel doesn't have to walk around it. Now show me the basement."

"The basement?"

"I need to know how far it extends and if so, if it's sturdy enough to hold up the weight of an addition. That's a serious matter of code regulations."

Thank God I just cleaned out the kitty litter boxes this morning, Jane thought to herself as she led him to the door of the basement.

Jack took lots of measurements and kept jotting down notes. Finally he said, "I'll have to measure upstairs from this door to be sure, but I don't think the basement will be relevant. It doesn't go as far as the dining room is my gut feeling. But let's go back upstairs."

He was well in front of them and went up the stairs faster than Jane had ever done.

After he measured, he said, "I'll take this back to my office and my son will put it on AutoCad."

"What's that?"

"A hideously expensive computer program that takes months to learn and is necessary to any architectural company. My son knows how to do this. Oh, and one more thing, where do the phone lines run in? I have to go outside and look. Mel, I assume you need a fast phone line for your computer and fax, and a separate line for telephone calls."

"I do."

"Where's the door to the backyard?"

Chapter

SIX

The third Women's Safety meeting was earlier than the ones before—at ten in the morning—and was about foreign travel. It was shorter than the others. Miss Welbourne went through the rules of how to behave, dress, and protect yourself, especially if you were traveling to a Muslim country. "Wear no jewelry. Don't even take it along, except for a cheap watch. Wear long sleeves, long skirts, and wear at least a scarf on your head.

"Don't meet the eyes of men. It's considered loose and trashy and you'll be taken for a prostitute. Eat daintily. Women aren't considered real people in the Muslim culture. Very few women are educated. Don't get roped into conversations about American values or anything political.

"You should really try to travel with another woman or if you're married, with your husband. You will be a lot safer. If you're with a tour group, obey everything the leader tells you. It's unwise to rent a car and go off on your own. If you get lost, you could put yourself in great danger.

"Try to learn a little of the language in advance. 'Please,' 'Thank you,' 'Excuse me.' And how to order food. Don't order any kind of spirits. If you take some along in your suitcase, drink only in the privacy of your room and be very careful not to leave any empty bottles in your room. Keep a set of paper bags and throw the empties away without being noticed."

Jane and Shelley tuned out. They had absolutely no plans to go to such hostile, dangerous countries. Miss Welbourne had a whole lot more advice. All of it was scary. Jane and Shelley were tempted to try to sneak out, but they'd be bound to be seen and didn't want to insult the teacher.

Jane occupied herself by thinking about the extra room she was adding for Mel's home office. It would raise her property taxes and probably her insurance rates as well. But there was no going back. Mel couldn't have worked in the sewing room, which was just big enough for one single bed and one small side table with barely room for a lamp, and had only one pitiful little window.

She hadn't even told Shelley about this. Shelley had been out and about shopping while Jack was there. She couldn't wait to tell her about it.

When the class was over, they went to their favorite

restaurant; they were early enough to get a booth where nobody could hear them talking.

Jane told Shelley about the house extension and Shelley said, "That's going to be a huge, expensive, messy project."

"But worth it, Shelley. Mel has a whole extra bedroom in his apartment with copies of his files, a computer, printer, two phone lines. He can't fit that in that extra room upstairs. He's going to move into my house and he deserves to be accommodated with all he needs."

"I see that. But won't it cost the earth?"

"So what? My pharmacy money is increasing every year as it expands."

"Speaking of the business, have you told Thelma that you're getting married?"

"Yes, and she chewed me out."

"How dare she!"

"Because she's old and nasty. She resents me for getting Steve's share of the profits forever, which will be passed on to my children when I'm gone. That's what is in his will."

Shelley asked, "Have you ever had their bookkeeping audited?"

Jane stared at her best friend. "No, I haven't. But I probably should. It would be like her to cheat me."

Jane thought for a minute or two and said, "But Steve's brother Ted is in charge of the finances. I don't think Ted would allow it. If she tried to fudge, he'd stop her because it might get him in legal trouble."

Shelley nodded approval. "Back to your extra room, how far along is this plan?"

"Uncle Jim added a room to his house and recommended an architect. A guy we're supposed to call Jack. He's already working on it. In fact, he insisted on visiting Mel's apartment to measure how much space he has there, so he could give him just as much at my house. He's an interesting old guy. Measured like mad. Went out in the backyard to see where the phone lines come in, checked out that there isn't any basement under where the new room will be."

"Meantime, you want to shop?"

"For what?"

"The bride outfit for Mel's mother Addie's wedding."

"Why not? I've thought about this a little. Mel wants me to wear that emerald suit that he likes so much in the real wedding before the showy one that Addie is trying to take over."

"What do you want? Ivory instead of white?"

"No. It's too close to white and would look merely dingy with the groom and best man in tuxes. I'm sure Addie is going to insist on this."

"Okay, let's go shopping again."

"We're starting at a place that supplies tuxes."

"Why?"

"Because I want to know if they have tuxes in a charcoal gray."

"You want to look like the groom and his best man?"

"No, I want to wear a brilliant red blouse and a classy

matching red hat, and Mel and whoever he chooses to stand up for him can wear ties and cummerbunds to match my hat and blouse. We've already struck out on pink and taupe."

"You're not old enough to wear a red hat," Shelley said firmly.

"Why not?"

"Because you're not fifty years old yet."

"Who made that rule?" Jane asked. "You?"

"The Red Hats Society. I think that's what they're called."

Jane sniffed and said, "You made that up. Admit it."

"No, I didn't. You can look it up on the Internet. The head of it is in her eighties I've been told. The local chapters 'Lunch,'" Shelley said, with verbal quotes around it. "Then there are big conventions that any member in good standing can attend."

"Beware! I'm going to look this group up on the Internet."

"Go ahead. By the way, is this color thing one of the rules you set up for Mel's mother?"

"Not really. But I did say she can't choose flocks of bridesmaids and groomsmen. By the time she realizes this, if we find what I want and make a down payment on the men's tuxes, it will be a fait accompli."

Jane called around and found a tux rental place that had the charcoal-colored tuxes and got a fabric sample. "I can't shop for the dress today, Shelley. I need to let Willard out in the yard. He hasn't been out since seven this morning."

Jane went home and she found Willard, her big old dog sitting by the back door, which he'd almost scratched clear through over the years. Instead of running outside barking as he'd usually done, he walked slowly into the backyard. And as he raised one leg to pee, he fell over.

Jane ran to him, her heart racing. He was lying on his side, his eyes open, and a little blood oozing out of his mouth. Jane ran back to the house and called Todd.

"Todd, I need help quickly. It's Willard. Get that old quilt he likes and put it in the back of the Jeep. We need to get him to the vet."

Todd had instead put Willard's old dog bed in the back of the Jeep and they both had to carry the heavy dog to the car. Jane drove almost as fast as Shelley did. And two of the girls at the front desk helped them carry Willard inside. Dr. Roberts was waiting and they laid the dog on the examining table. The doctor got out his stethoscope and put it on Willard's chest. "How did this happen?" he asked Jane.

She told him.

"He was probably dead before he hit the ground. A merciful sudden death. He didn't feel anything. You know he had an enlarged heart for the last several years."

"Can we take him home and bury him in the yard?" Todd asked.

"There's probably some health code that forbids this," the doctor said. "How about this: we'll cremate him and put his ashes in a little enclosed box? Then you can get one of those kits for making concrete stepping-stones to write on. You can write his name on it and the date of his birth and death."

"You know his date of birth?" Jane asked through her tears.

"Of course. Remember you adopted him here. Willard's mother was a car chaser and was killed when her two puppies were ten weeks old. They were brought here so they could be adopted. It's all in my file. I'll write down the date. You subtract ten weeks. Todd and Ms. Jeffry, he was loved by the whole family. He had a good long happy life. Keep that in mind."

He shook Todd's hand and held it with both of his. "He was a good dog. I know you'll miss him."

They left behind the dog bed and were both crying on the way home. To Jane's knowledge Todd hadn't cried since he was eight when Thelma's husband died and they had attended his funeral.

As the doctor had suggested they stopped by a hobby store and bought the kit for the stepping-stone. Jane thought that making the stone now might ease Todd's grief.

Janie had suspected for the last few weeks that Willard wouldn't be with them for much longer. He'd been sleeping too much, not eating his food as fast. And not running around the yard barking at imaginary predators on his turf. She'd soon lose her old cats as well. They were nearly as old as Willard.

She wondered if the cats would miss Willard as much as his people would. Probably so.

Chapter

SEVEN

When Jane got back from the vet, she had a blinking message from the architect on her phone. "Jane, this is Jack. I forgot to tell you something. When we get approval for this project, we'll have to take part of your south fence out to get the equipment into your backyard. I noticed that you have a dog. So take it outside on a leash when we're ready."

She didn't have the heart to call back and say she no longer had the old dog. Even though she was curious about when the pouring of the foundation would start. She'd ask him later.

Nor was she calm enough yet to tell Katie and Mike. She did call Shelley, who sympathized in the best way. "That's the thing about well-loved pets. We always outlive them. I suppose the worst scenario is that one would outlive us and have to go to strangers."

"Thanks, Shelley. You're right. I'm never getting a dog again. It's too hard to lose one. The same with cats. Well, not exactly. They don't really need you to be home all the time. Leave lots of kitty litter and food and water and go away for a weekend and they're mildly happy when you get home. Dogs aren't like that. They love their people and are sad when they're left alone, or—God forbid—put in a kennel."

"There is another difference," Shelley said. "Dogs love their owners. Cats think they own you."

Jane laughed and then went on to tell Shelley how nice the vet had been, especially to Todd. The vet took so much trouble to comfort Todd on Willard's death, and explained about the headstone idea.

"He's such a nice man," Shelley said. "We had always taken our pets to him back when we had pets. He cared about them and their owners, even though one of our cats' records was headed 'Caution—Mean Cat.'"

That made Jane laugh again. She vaguely remembered that cat of the Nowacks'. It had bitten both her and Mike the first time each of them had tried to pet it.

"You really need to go shopping tomorrow for your dress for the fake wedding," Shelley said.

"That sounds like excellent therapy."

They took along the scrap of charcoal fabric they'd talked the tux guy into finding. But after two complete rounds of trampling entirely through three dress stores, found nothing even close.

"Don't worry, Jane. A fabric store will have an exact match and I know an excellent dressmaker who can make whatever you need."

"Right now what I need most is to go home and see if Todd has finished his headstone for Willard. Todd will want me to compliment it the moment he finishes and his feelings will be hurt if I'm not there."

Shelley, who'd often been in similar situations with her children when pets had died, agreed. "We have lots of time. Neither wedding is for a few months. Give me that scrap of fabric and I'll go through every fabric store in town like Sherman through Altanta."

Todd had finished the headstone and did a good job of it.

"How did you get all that writing so neat?" Jane asked.

"With one of my pens that was out of ink."

In large letters at the top it said WILLARD. Below that were the dates of his birth and death. At the bottom Todd had drawn quite an accurate drawing of the dog in his prime. He'd even colored it in.

"That's a fine job. Are you going to varnish it so it won't fade or run?"

"I hadn't thought about that. That's a good idea. But it needs to dry completely before I do it. It's still a bit damp."

"I need to call Mike and Katie with the bad news. They're going to be as sad as we are."

Todd looked away. "I'll do it if you want. I've been remembering when he was a puppy and I wanted him to sleep in my bed with me and you wouldn't let me because I might roll over and squash him. So he had a little bed next to mine. You made him a nice soft cushion to sleep on."

"I remember. He was a cute puppy, wasn't he? Who'd have guessed then how big and strong he'd get," Jane said. "And remember how soft his fur was? Everybody wanted to cuddle him."

Todd was obviously feeling better, having this talk with his mother. Earlier today she'd been so strong about it. Helping carry Willard to the car, and explaining to the vet how he'd died. Jane was glad she'd come home to have this time with Todd.

"Would you rather I called Katie and Mike?" he suddenly asked.

"I'd like it if you would. But if you get an answering machine, though, don't leave a message except to call home."

He cocked a cynical eyebrow. "Mom, I'm not a dim bulb."

She laughed. "I know that. I shouldn't have warned you. I'll leave you to it and not eavesdrop. I'll make a cup of coffee and sit on the patio."

As she sat outside, she realized that Todd had reached the cusp between childhood and being an adult. It was, as she well remembered, one of the milestones of most people's lives. Scary but exciting doing the balancing act. Offering to give the bad news to his older sister and brother and sparing his mother was a big step forward.

The next morning Jane received another call from the architect. "Did you get my message about your dog?"

"Yes, but when you called, we had him at the vet. He's dead. Heart attack."

There was a silence and Jack cleared his throat. "I'm so sorry to have asked such a tactless question. Your uncle Jim would be ashamed of me."

"Don't worry. You had no way to know. I wanted you to realize why I hadn't been polite enough to reply. Do you have any idea when the work can start?"

"Very soon. At least by next Tuesday or Wednesday if it's to be done before your wedding."

"I'm surprised. Yes, that would be wonderful if it could happen."

"I can't promise that the small things will be finished by then. Cleaning the windows, finishing the trim and such. But it will be a livable, usable area by the time you're back from your honeymoon," he added with a chuckle.

Jane realized that she and Mel hadn't even discussed having a honeymoon. How could either of them get away from work? Mel was virtually always on call and Jane had some work to do on the almost finished second book. She wanted to get it in well before the deadline, which was two weeks before the real wedding. She'd more or less thought that with the kids home for the wedding, her parents visiting after a long flight, and a fair amount of stress to get Mel's room ready, that they might just spend one glorious night at a really good hotel and spend the next few days relaxing with family and friends.

Besides, a honeymoon for middle-aged people, not that either she or Mel thought of themselves as such, was a bit silly.

Though she was in contact at least twice a week with her parents via e-mail, it would be nice to sit around the kitchen table just talking to them. Or take them to restaurants, and see some new sights that had sprung up all over the Chicago area since they'd last been here.

Then she thought of her sister, Marty. She and Marty were like oil and water. They'd never shared common interests or values. Marty had been married at least four times. They hadn't laid eyes on each other for well over a decade. More likely two decades. Jane realized that Marty hadn't ever met Mike, Katie, and Todd. She had no interest in children. They didn't exchange birthday or holiday cards or gifts.

Jane was also afraid to invite Marty, because she always had an inappropriate man, to say the least, living with her. The only reason Jane knew this was because Marty was always nagging their parents to help support the current husband or boyfriend. She never succeeded and never gave up trying.

Jane also knew that her parents, who complained about Marty, never told Marty anything about Jane or her family. Marty never asked. It was as if she'd forgotten she ever had a sister. She'd have to e-mail her folks to see if there was any slim chance they wanted their other daughter at the wedding. She was sure she knew the answer. But it was the polite thing to ask them anyway.

She was happily distracted from all these worries by Shelley knocking at the kitchen door. Shelley was carrying a big paper bag with paper handles that were about to give up the ghost.

"Come in. What's all this?"

"Fabrics," Shelley said grimly. "Clear your dining room table."

"There's nothing on it now except a tablecloth," Jane replied.

With a flourish Shelley dumped a good fifty strips about four inches wide and twelve inches long on the table.

"Jeepers!" Jane exclaimed with a laugh. "You didn't mix up the charcoal piece I got at the tux place, did you?"

"Ye of little faith. No, that one's in my purse. We'll put it at the end of the table so we don't lose it."

They started pawing through the samples of fabric. "This checkerboard thing won't do," Jane said.

"Nor will the lumpy black-and-white."

They threw both on the floor.

Sadly, as they went on, nearly everything went onto the floor. There were only two pieces of fabric of the fifty that almost matched, but not quite.

"If you want dark, you're going to have to go with pure black," Shelley said.

"Sounds like one of those old trashy paperback mysteries written by men in the 1930s. *The Bride Wore Black*."

"If you wore a black long skirt and short jacket with a bright red blouse, would that do?"

"All the people behind me at the church wedding are just going to see the black. There's tan, of course. And the groomsmen would look like they were National Guard guys."

"White?" Shelley suggested with a disgusted shrug.

"No, no, no."

"Pink?"

"Too girly-girly," Jane said.

"Bright red, then?"

"Floozy."

"Carmine red?"

Jane paused. "Maybe." She laughed. "Mel's mother will probably fall into a faint as I come down the aisle."

Chapter

EIGHT

On Monday Jane got back to work, tweaking her manuscript, and double checking her historical research and punctuation. She hadn't yet figured out the exact dates and what days they fell on but she had a bookmark on her computer for any month of any year you wanted to look up. She might have to adjust a few things considering that her heroine was a churchgoer.

Since Todd had grown up, he'd decided that Sunday school was too childish and church services were too boring. And Jane herself had more or less given up as well. She'd only gone to church to set a good example for the children and the church that they'd always gone to was turning quite a bit to the fundamentalist view-point anyway. And anytime lately that she had showed up, somebody tried to buttonhole her to run some sort of fund-raising project.

She pulled up a bookmark for the year she needed and made a printout of the four months the story involved. Later she'd cut them out and enlarge each one on her copier and thumbtack them to her bulletin board.

The phone rang as she was printing out the year she was working on. "Hello, Jack, what's up?"

"You need to hire a contractor. Your uncle Jim liked the one he chose. You should talk to him. Or get another bid on the advice of someone else you trust. But whoever you choose should be ready to start on the foundation next week on Tuesday or Wednesday. It involves digging a huge hole, filling it with gravel, and building wooden barriers for foundation pouring. For a while it will be noisy, especially when the concrete truck pulls into your side yard. Your contractor should do that because there are no gardens on that end of the yard. You might want to keep your cats inside when the concrete is poured so they don't bring it in the house if they explore it."

"I'll call Uncle Jim right now."

When he answered, she heard the faint whirring sound of some sort of machine turning off. "Uncle Jim, Jack Edgeworth told me to talk to you about the contractor you used."

"He's John Beckman. He was good. Knows all the good subcontractors, all the county and township codes, and goes and gets the right permits for every stage of the work."

"Mr. Edgeworth suggested I get a second bid from

someone I trust. But you're the only one I can think of trusting."

"That's nice of you to say. Here is his telephone number."

"Thanks. I'll call him immediately."

She did so, and found the man pleasant and agreeable to starting the work the next week, which surprised her.

I must finish this book before this starts, Jane thought. A good incentive to get it in earlier than she needed to send it to her agent to read before it was sent on to the publisher. No more messing around trying to find a wedding dress or considering colors to wear for a fake wedding for the time being.

By Monday afternoon, Jane had been to the FedEx box to deposit the manuscript into the maw of it. She stood for a minute, enjoying the sound of it thumping on the bottom of the metal box on its way to New York.

She'd need to start a third book soon. At least start making notes about possible characters, especially the main character. She'd need a new setting. The one she'd just completed had taken place considerably later than the first. What other area of American history did she want to pursue? Revolutionary times? Colonial?

She'd already accumulated quite a library of costumes through time, styles of housing, important dates, words and phrases, dictionaries, and even a book of inventions and when the new technologies had originated. She had a seven-language dictionary, a bird and butterfly guide, as well as one about wild animals so she wouldn't make errors about where they lived in various seasons.

But the historical time lines were the best. She might drop by a bookstore while the noise was going on and see if there was some new book that would be useful. After all, she'd learned at a mystery writers and readers conference that books were deductible if you were a writer. She wondered if her cable bills would count. She'd taken notes from lots of programs on the History Channel. She'd check with her accountant. After all, deductions, as Martha Stewart was always saying, were a Good Thing.

Jane invited Todd to go along.

"I like books and bookstores, but you take so much time that I go crazy. I'll pass this time."

Jane was relieved. She knew she spent too much time when she went to a big bookstore. She was greedy for books. She'd take a list of the subjects, but didn't include mysteries. Those were the shelves she browsed through first before she could even consider the research books.

She found some of her favorites. Charlaine Harris had a new hardback and a paperback on the shelves. She hadn't read either of them yet. Rhys Bowen had a new paperback historical mystery so she picked that up as well. Jill Churchill had another of her books set in the thirties she couldn't resist.

She'd read these in the evenings when she'd finished her own work for the day. Then she consulted her list.

She'd looked up the latest *USA Today* booklist of the 150 bestsellers that week and taken notes. She'd also just browsed all of the nonfiction and history sections. She kept piling up books at a desk in the middle of the store, putting a sticky note on the top saying "Save for Jane Jeffry."

She had to have two bags because one would have spilled its guts out the bottom before she could haul it to the car. The real treasure she found was a government study of the most popular names for boys and girls through the whole last century. It listed the thirty most popular for each year. A plethora of names. Unfortunately, most of them for decades were Mary and John. But there were some really good ones that cropped up occasionally. Carmina, Drew, Mick, Serena, and for a spell after the last version of the movie about the *Titanic* came out, there were lots and lots of first place Jacks and Roses.

Early Tuesday morning Jane was awoken by the sound of her fence coming down. She'd forgotten to buy kitty litter and bins to see if they still remembered what they were for. She made a quick run to a pet store and discovered there was now a wonderful thing called "self-clumping kitty litter." Everything, including liquid, turned into a ball. You bought scoops with grooves through them, and lots of plastic bags. She was also told to get a box of baking soda and a fine sieve. Stir a tiny bit in every time you cleaned out the clumps and they wouldn't smell bad—to the cats or the person cleaning up. The pet store manager suggested that she should buy two low-sided bins. Most cats didn't want to use each other's bins.

When she returned home, she found a good-sized

plastic container in an upper cabinet that would do for a generous water bowl. There was lots of noise outside and the cats had taken refuge in the basement, just as they always did during lightning storms.

Todd and Shelley's boy John were already outside loving the noise and lots of strong men with power tools.

Jane made earplugs out of wadded-up tissues, and took her embarrassingly big bags of books outside to arrange them on the patio table in the shade of the umbrella. She laid them all out and started looking them over, one by one. There were very noisy digging machines carrying away a huge amount of soil and putting it into equally noisy trucks that took the dirt away. At the end of the day, there was an enormous hole in the backyard. At least four feet deep.

The next day, she was out early to see what was going on next and found that work had stopped and there was a calico cat with two kittens looking down into the hole. The mother was meowing loudly and there was a sound of mewing coming out of the hole. A workman got in the hole and after a bit of a chase, lifted the little orange kitten out.

The mother immediately started almost brutally washing the kitten, one paw holding it down. When the orange kitten was clean, she walked serenely out of the area of missing fence at the north end of the yard, three kittens running to catch up with her. Jane was smiling when the man who had rescued the kitten approached her.

"We need to go into your basement to drill through for hot water, cold water, and hook up to the sewer line."

"I'll have to get my own cats locked up or you'll be stepping on them. They're very curious."

"That's fine. My workers need to get their tools out of the truck."

Jane hauled the kitty litter bins, a bowl of water, and cat food up to her bathroom, then went back down to fetch Max and Meow.

By the time she returned there were horrible drilling noises coming from the basement again, and she went out to look down the hole.

There were four men in it now, one was helping thread the pipes through from the basement, and the others were building restraining walls to keep the concrete from flowing over the yard, she assumed. But the hole would take tons and tons of concrete. Wouldn't it be so heavy that the entire addition would gradually sink into the hole?

The general contractor had arrived and was watching the workmen. She approached him and asked him about her fears of the whole thing sinking. He laughed and said, "It won't be filled with concrete. It will be mostly gravel with a vapor barrier over it."

As he was explaining, a pipe appeared coming through the foundation closest to the far wall of the hole. "Which one is that?" Jane asked.

"Hot water," he said as somebody else in the hole was connecting a black pipe with a curve at the bottom and coming up very high. "It has to be higher than usual and all of them will be capped off higher than necessary."

"Why are they coming out from the dining room foundation?"

"Because you don't want anything that holds water on an outside wall or it could freeze and burst."

Jane almost said "Duh" but John Beckman was used to people who hadn't added a room before asking silly questions.

By the time all the pipes were installed and capped off, she went to free the cats. When she got back downstairs, there were four men with heavily loaded bags of gravel in wheelbarrows. They were all sweating like pigs.

Others were building walls with big boards around the perimeter of the hole.

Jane was again sitting at the patio table under the umbrella. Todd and Shelley's son were also watching every step. Now and then, Jane would look up and see how the boards that would prevent the concrete from running all over the place were coming along. The workers were fast and efficient. They drove steel spikes into the ground every few feet to, presumably, keep the weight of the concrete from pushing the boards out of alignment.

By noon one and a half sections of wood were already in, and watching all the leveling, it looked as if it was going to be a good flat area to pour the concrete (or was the proper word cement?) nice and flat. She'd have to ask about the right word.

She went inside to make sandwiches for Todd and

John and checked the kitty litter. One or the other of the cats had availed itself of one of the bins. Cats always seemed to her to have very short memories. But apparently they had some sort of early memory of kitty litter from kittenhood. She tried out the sieve. It worked like a charm. She scattered a half teaspoon of baking soda over the area of the bin that had been used and with the fine sieve mixed it in. Then she put the plastic bag with the solid lump into the trash bin behind the garage.

From now on, this could be a job for Todd. In fact, as old as the cats were, they might as well turn back into indoor cats, as they had been when they were kittens. On the other hand, climbing that fence kept them from clawing sofas and chairs. Maybe she'd just check the kitty litter after rainstorms when all this work was done.

She came upstairs, washed her hands, and went back outside to fondle her stash of new books.

By late Thursday, the wooden barrier was in place. The gravel was all in the hole with vapor barrier over it, and by Friday the concrete truck arrived. It backed halfway over her front lawn and a long sturdy hose was attached to the back and snaked around to the far corner of the wooden enclosure. With a horrific groan, the truck started to pump out thick gray stuff while a whole new crew of workers shoveled and troweled as more and more arrived. From the far corner to the corner closest, the house was complete in a mere few hours.

Jane had pictured a fleet of wheelbarrows carrying loads and loads of it and dropping nasty glops onto the grass in her front yard. Times had certainly changed since she and Steve had watched the basement floor going in the big hole.

She called Mel and said, "Come over after work and see the beginning of your office. It's gorgeous. So smooth. And so quick to be poured through a big tube."

"I have some paperwork that I have to turn in by five-thirty. Why don't you call in an order for pick-up at our favorite Chinese restaurant at quarter of six and I'll get it on the way over?"

"Sounds good. What do you want?"

"The same thing I always get."

This meant spicy Mongolian beef with shrimp fried rice.

Chapter

NINE

Jane had slept late on Tuesday. When Shelley phoned her, she almost fell out of bed trying to find out who was calling.

"Jane, you were asleep, weren't you?" Shelley accused.

"As a matter of fact, I was. I had a bad dream about something I don't remember and couldn't get back to sleep for hours. Must have been something I ate last night."

"You've forgotten we have an appointment this morning?"

"I guess I have."

"It's our next safety meeting. It's at ten. It's nine-thirty now. Want me to go without you?"

"I think you better. I'll come along as soon as I can."

Jane dressed hastily, tried to get her hair under control,

slapped on makeup, and yelled at Todd that she was leaving for a meeting.

She had trouble finding her car keys, but located them under a chair in the kitchen and set out. She wasn't going to drive fast. She wished, in fact, that she'd just begged off, making up a stomach upset or head-banging migraine.

As she came around the last turn looking for a parking space, the street was full of emergency equipment. An ambulance, a fire truck, several police cars. She managed an illegal U-turn and parked around the corner.

Shelley must have seen her do it. She met Jane at the corner. "I'm sorry I made you come. I'm more sorry that I came."

"What's happened here? It looks as if everybody is going in and out of the meeting place for the class."

"A woman at the community meeting place is dead. Another woman in the class came in early and discovered that the door to the meeting was slightly open. She found her in the meeting room."

A few other members of the class were standing around or sitting on the front steps. Two police officers, one in uniform and Mel VanDyne, were questioning the woman. She was sitting with her feet in the gutter across the street, sobbing.

"Is that the woman called Doris?" Jane asked.

"I think that was her name, but I didn't take notes."

Jane realized that Mel had noticed them. He turned

away from the sobbing woman and made a slight shooing gesture.

Neither of them wanted to look like bloodthirsty snoops, as did most of the other people looking from windows and doors along the street, so Jane and Shelley were quick to go back to their cars.

"You parked illegally," Shelley said.

"I did?"

"See that yellow ticket on your windshield? You didn't put money in the parking meter."

"Rats," Jane said. "Don't tell Mel. Or our sons."

They went home. Jane wrote a check for the parking ticket and put it out with the mail. She took several of her books she'd recently bought outside with a bunch of sticky notes to mark pages she thought might have interesting material. There wasn't anything going on with the room addition today. The concrete was setting up and it would be next week before anything else could be done.

"Until we have a firm base, we can't proceed. By Monday we'll be back," the contractor said.

Jane had taken her cell phone outside again. It was a mild day under the umbrella and she liked sitting in the shade. If Mel had anything he could tell her about what had happened that morning at the Women's Safety meeting place, he could reach her. Apparently something awful had been done to someone. There was no way to even guess who it was. She hoped it wasn't Miss Welbourne. She wasn't really fond of the woman, but Miss Welbourne was doing a good, knowledgeable service for a lot of women. It had already been enlightening for Jane and Shelley. The stuff about protecting your belongings in a purse was good advice. Looking brave and alert if you found yourself in a scary neighborhood was also advice that she'd remember.

As she expected, Mel didn't contact her. She and Shelley decided to watch the local news at five and see if something was mentioned.

But Shelley caught a newscast at noon and came over to tell Jane what she'd heard.

"They just said that a freelance teacher had been murdered overnight on that block. The police weren't yet giving out the name or circumstances nor anything about the murder weapon or suspects."

"It does sound as if it might have been Miss Welbourne, doesn't it?" Jane asked.

"Unless there is another teacher in an adjoining classroom who was the victim," Shelley suggested.

"I suppose that's possible. But I didn't see any bulletin board notes about other classes being held there today. Did you?"

"I didn't really pay attention," Shelley admitted. "And there is no way the police are going to let us in the building to look."

"And it's really not any of our business," Jane added, but she was as curious as Shelley was.

"What are all those sticky notes bristling from that pile of books for?" Shelley asked, sitting down on a patio chair.

"Just things that might be useful to plot my next book."

"Can't you take a little time off?"

"I could. But I don't want to. I sent in the second one the other day."

"You didn't mention that to me." Shelley sounded a bit irritated.

"You knew I was almost done. I didn't think you needed to know where and when I mailed it in."

Shelley grinned. "You're right. I'm not your mother."

Mel called Jane late in the afternoon. "I was glad to see that you and Shelley took my gesture to go back home so well."

"What happened and to whom?" Jane asked.

"Miss Welbourne was murdered."

"When?"

"We don't know yet. In fact we know very little so far. I just wanted you to know. I have to go now. If I learn anything else I'll let you know."

It was late the next day when Mel got back to Jane. "Sorry for the delay. Your uncle Jim was in charge of the case against the man who killed his wife, who was a member of that class. It was easy to get him. Then Miss Welbourne was murdered as well and Jim handed it off to me."

"That's understandable, isn't it?"

"Of course it was. I'm not complaining. Jim's perp was

in jail and is about the only person who couldn't be the perpetrator. It's impossible for him to have killed Miss Welbourne."

"So what do you know so far?"

"Not much. The pathologist said at first that she'd been hit on the front of her head. He's not even sure whether she was alive or dead when it happened. If she'd had a stroke or a heart attack within a moment of the attack it would be hard to know. What is clear is that she didn't get the injury by herself. She wasn't found near anything that she could have struck her head against in a fall. No sign of blood on any piece of furniture. No weapon found nearby, or near the site."

"Thanks for letting me know. You'll solve it, of course."

"Or the pathologist will find more evidence of the cause of death."

Jane called Shelley and reported what Mel had said.

"It's a shame that someone who taught women to protect themselves had to die. Was it a natural death?"

"Mel said they didn't know yet. The pathologist hasn't determined yet if she had a stroke or heart attack before or after someone hit her in the head."

"So if she could have survived the stroke or heart attack, and someone found her quickly enough, she might have lived. Otherwise it's murder," Shelley said bluntly.

"I suppose so."

"I wish we could at least see her notes of what she meant

to talk about today. It had to be more interesting than the last session about traveling to foreign countries."

Jane said, "I'd guess every scrap of paper in the room has been seized, and is unavailable to us. At least for now."

"Ask Mel about it, would you? Not right now but later."

"Will do."

Jane had barely put the phone down when she had a call from her mother-in-law, Thelma.

"Jane, I'd like to get together with you at some nice restaurant the day after tomorrow to talk about your wedding. I've already picked out a nice place." She gave the name of the restaurant and directions and set a time and told Jane that she'd make the reservation momentarily.

"And dress well, if you would," Thelma added.

Jane was tempted to scream, but said calmly, "I always dress nicely to go to good restaurants."

"I've seen you at nice restaurants wearing blue jeans."

Jane had to laugh. "Thelma nobody but you calls them 'blue' jeans anymore. If I wore jeans, they'd be expensive designer jeans. And by the way, where did you see me in jeans?"

There was a moment of silence, then Thelma said, "It wasn't really me who saw you. It was a woman from the church who knew you when you were still going to church."

Another criticism. Two in a row.

"I've written it down in my date book. I'll meet you there."

Jane immediately called Shelley back.

"You've finally decided on what you're wearing to the fake wedding?"

"No. Nothing like that. I just had an unpleasant call from Thelma."

"Aren't all Thelma's conversations unpleasant?"

"Yes, but this one has me worried. She's up to something that's sure to be really nasty. Let's go to a restaurant for lunch," Jane suggested.

They'd made sure to sit far away from the other diners so they wouldn't be overheard. Jane repeated what Thelma said.

"Dress well!" Shelley exclaimed. Then she sat back a bit from the table, thinking. "I don't buy the story about the church lady seeing you."

"Neither do I."

"A private detective?"

"Exactly what I guessed," Jane said. "But why?"

"Just general snooping?"

"Thelma doesn't spend money out of sheer curiosity."

"Trying to find out something bad about you?"

"I assume so. But what good would it do her? I'm not aware of doing anything absurd or illegal in a restaurant or anywhere else in public. What's she hoping to learn about my private life?" Jane mused.

"I guess you'll have to show up to find out. Jane, she's up to no good, that's for sure. By the way, you need to make a decision soon about what you are wearing for the fake wedding. Have you invited Thelma to either or both?"

"Informally. I told her there would be a civil ceremony

and another in a church or hotel. I didn't explain why, but said she would be welcome to come to either or both."

"And she said?"

"That she'd think about it when I sent her a proper invitation."

"I wish I could be a fly on the wall," Shelley said. "Call me the moment your luncheon with Thelma is over."

Jane made a point of being early to arrive at the restaurant so she could choose a table where they could eat and speak in privacy. Jane was wearing a black skirt, hose, and heels and a bright yellow short-sleeved summer sweater. She went to wait at the bar and smoke one of her rare cigarettes to fortify herself. She'd already put it out, paid for her drink and the tip, when Thelma marched in the door.

The waiter showed them to the corner booth. Thelma was dressed in her old-fashioned best, clutching a big purse and a maroon leather folder, which she put down next to her chair.

"It's been a long time since we've seen each other," she said accusingly.

"Only a month ago," Jane reminded her. "I had you and Ted, Dixie, and their darling little girls for Todd's birthday."

Thelma frowned. "So silly of them to take on those Chinese babies. How can they pretend they gave birth to them?"

"I doubt they're pretending any such thing," Jane said.

Ted, Jane's much younger brother-in-law, and his wife, Dixie, had been trying to have babies ever since Jane's kids were in grade school and never managed it. Jane admired them for finally, almost middle-aged, going to China to bring those pretty little sisters home with them. Jane thought they were adorable. Naturally this got Thelma's goat. Chinese granddaughters had never been among her priorities. They weren't "like us" she'd said at the birthday party in front of everyone. "They have straight black hair and funny-looking eyes."

Jane, fuming over the memory, studied her menu.

Thelma said, "I see you've already bought a drink."

"It's just a mild Chianti. I won't get falling-down drunk, if that was what you're implying."

Thelma glared at her. "I'll just have coffee."

The waiter then took their food orders. Jane asked for a simple shrimp salad. Thelma ordered a chicken pot pie. The restaurant was famous for their pot pies done with real puff pastry and delicious vegetables and interesting spices.

"While we eat, I'll come to the point," Thelma said picking up the leather folder and bringing out a document.

Thelma's copy of Steve's will. What on earth was she up to? Jane wondered.

Thelma handed it over. "Take a look at this."

"I don't need to," Jane said. "I have my own copy in my lockbox at the bank."

"Look through it anyway," Thelma ordered.

Stapled to the back page was a typed notice of an

amendment saying, "Should Jane remarry, this contract becomes null and void." There was Steve's signature below it, and two church ladies' signatures as witnesses.

Jane's first impulse was to laugh at Thelma's incompetence, but she said quietly, "That's not anything like Steve's signature. You wrote it. You are a forger. And this is typed on that fake handwriting typewriter I gave you years ago. I'm going to audit the company books. If you dare try to enforce this, I'll take you to court and you'll either go to jail or be laughed out of court as a demented old woman and a forger. That's a crime."

Jane fished in her purse and threw down a twenty-dollar bill and a five. "This will pay for my lunch with a good tip. You can take my salad home to eat yourself."

Jane rose and walked out of the restaurant without looking back.

"NO!" Shelley exclaimed.

She put her head down on her kitchen table, half laughing, half enraged.

"Yes. A forged addendum to Steve's will. I threatened to take her to court and hire an auditor to go over her books. I need to call Ted and warn him about this. I don't want him to think I distrust him."

Shelley sat back up. "Can you conduct an audit?"

"Why not?"

"I think you'd have to get a court order or something. You're not a partner."

"But I am. I'm listed in the real will as 'his third share in perpetuity should he predecease me per stirpes should we have children.'"

"What's per stirpes?"

"By natural birth, as opposed to adoption. We didn't even have children when this was written. Nor did he plan to die before me. I threatened Thelma with going to jail for forgery."

"You didn't!"

"I did. And I'll do it if she tries to pull this off. The awful woman."

Shelley grinned. "You should lock your mother-in-law and Mel's mother in a room and wait and see who comes out alive."

Jane laughed. "What fun that would be."

"So you just walked out on her?"

"I threw down a twenty and a five and told her to take my meal home when it came and walked straight out of the restaurant."

"You're a better woman than I am," Shelley said. "I'd have thrown a glass of ice water in her face first."

"She'd have had me arrested for assault." Jane giggled. "At least I gave Thelma a good scare. I forgot to mention that she doesn't seem to consider Ted and Dixie's children as her grandchildren. When Ted and Dixie brought them to dinner for Todd's birthday, she acted as if they weren't even there."

"Why not? Because they're Chinese?"

"Of course. She's a bigot as well as a forger."

"Jane, how have you managed to put up with her for all these years?"

"The same way you put up with Paul's sister Constanza. She's the same kind of snoopy, overbearing woman. We could put Thelma, Addie, and Constanza in a locked room and see which one comes out alive."

Shelley laughed and said, "So you didn't eat lunch. Neither have I. Let's go back to the restaurant and gorge."

"What if Thelma's still there?"

"Who cares?"

"You're right. I was really looking forward to that shrimp salad I ordered."

Thelma had left and both Jane and Shelley had the shrimp salad. Unfortunately the same waiter who had earlier taken Jane's order took the same order again. Seeing his confusion, Jane said, "I had an emergency call on my cell phone and had to leave. The emergency is over. I hope the lady I was with took my order home."

"So she did," the waiter said. "And she looked quite angry as she left."

Jane didn't speak until he was gone and grinned at Shelley. "Mad as a hornet."

When they'd both finished eating, Shelley said, not surprisingly, "Let's go shopping for what you want to wear for your other mother-in-law's wedding."

They found a long, slim black almost floor-length silk skirt that fit Jane perfectly. She wanted to see it at least three times from the back. "That's the view the whole audience will see."

To their delight, the clerk tapped at the dressing room door and said, "There is a matching jacket for this. Would you like to see it?"

"Oh yes," the two of them said in unison.

The clerk returned with the jacket in two sizes. The first looked droopy. The second was perfect. Cut in a princess style to show off that she still had a waist, she said, "I'll take this, too. Thank you."

Shelley said, "You haven't even looked at the price tags."

"I hope both are expensive. It would make me happy to spend what Thelma thinks I wouldn't be able to afford if she'd put herself in such a greedy, grasping plot to take away my third of the pharmacy profits."

Shelley grinned. "You're absolutely right, Jane. Now let's see if we can find a blouse in carmine red while you're in a throwing-away money mode."

They failed to find the right blouse at the store where they got the suit, and Jane said, "That's okay. In fact, it's a good thing. We should have checked at the tux place to see if they have carmine cummerbunds. Or we could make some to match when we do find the right blouse. But we could pick the shoes today."

"I don't think so. We probably need to make sure you have the right color carmine shoes."

Chapter

TEN

They struck out on finding a good blouse and Jane said, "I'm sick to death of shopping. Maybe I have something at home I could wear."

This turned out to be every bit as fruitless as shopping, but Jane made the best of it and purged a lot of things she hadn't worn for at least three years.

"Jane, that's a great skirt and jacket but you look more like a widow than a bride, to tell the truth. It would be great for a cocktail party."

"But I *am* a widow."

"Of course you are. But for this ceremony you should look like a bride, not a widow."

"You're right. But I might take this outfit back. I'm never invited to cocktail parties."

"Neither am I, except for Paul's meetings with his managers. But it would be great for fancy dinners, and it really flatters you."

Jane sat down on the heap of clothing now on her bed waiting to be recycled to a battered women's shelter and said, "Okay. I've made a nondecision decision. I'm keeping the skirt and jacket and I'm wearing the emerald dress to both the real and fake wedding. Mel loves it when I wear that dress and very few people will know I'd already worn it for the civil wedding. And we can forget all about matching fabrics for the cummerbunds for the tuxes."

With this shopping victory stalled out for all time, Jane was relieved that she could get on with real life. Going out to lunches with Shelley or dinners with Mel, doing research for her next book, gawking at the rapid progress of the room addition. She also kept asking the workers questions about what they were doing. They were kind to her. She brought them iced tea and sodas to ensure they'd remain tolerant of her.

The room was almost starting to look like a room, not a place to roller skate. Timbers were going up, firmly attached to the foundation.

She was told that electricity had to be next. There were several copies of Jack's blueprints. The overall structure. Where electrical lines went. Where windows of precise dimensions would be put in were marked as such. Where phone lines went. There were even water and sewer lines chalked out so Mel could have his own bathroom and sink.

Jack himself was there for at least an hour every day, overseeing the work. Sometimes he stayed longer.

"This is the fastest, most professional crew I've ever had the luck to put to work. A few of them are new to me, Jane."

He looked so smug about this that Jane was compelled to compliment him. And she meant it, too. He cared about how his projects turned out, and zealously pursued a timely, perfect completion.

"Your workers have been very polite about my uninformed questions."

"I know. They say you're the nicest lady most of them have ever worked for."

Jane actually simpered at the compliment. But she added, "There's a truck behind my car and I need to run an errand. Could you ask someone to move it? I'll park mine on the street when I get back."

She drove to the nearest public phone she could find and called her brother-in-law Ted. She feared that Thelma might be around and see the caller ID of her home phone.

"Ted, it's Jane. Don't say anything. Just let me ask you a favor. Your mother has forged a codicil to Steve's will cutting me out if I remarry."

Ted said, as if this was an ordinary business call, "That doesn't surprise me."

"Furthermore, I suspect she's hired a detective to keep track of where I go and how I'm dressed."

Ted's response was simply, "Ah."

"Here's what I'd like to do," Jane said. "Meet with me at the McDonald's down the street to the north of my house. You get there by eleven-thirty and I'll arrive ten or fifteen minutes later. Surely if there is a detective following me, he won't bother to come inside."

"Done."

When Jane arrived Ted was sitting as far from a window as it was possible to be. She joined him.

"Was someone following you?" he asked.

"There was a black car parked down the block that turned in here just two cars behind mine."

"Jane, I can't tell you how sorry I am. My mother should be put away somewhere. She's always been a rude woman. Now she's out of control. Right in front of our daughters she called our girls 'Chinks' without realizing how offensive it was. Poor Dixie cried all night. But I knew that my mother wouldn't be able to negate the adoption of the girls. Every single step was done correctly."

"I'm sorry for you, too, Ted. You have to spend a lot more time with her than I do. And thank goodness the girls aren't old enough or know enough English words to realize they had been insulted."

"It's getting harder and harder to put up with her," he admitted. "Dixie says she'll never allow my mother to be around the girls again, and I agree."

He went on, "As for the detective, I think I can easily put a stop to it. I do my mother's taxes every year and keep her checkbook balanced monthly, and this year there was a suspicious check for a thousand dollars that she wouldn't explain. She just said it was none of my business. But I still have the check in the file and it was endorsed by a detective agency. I thought at first she'd hired them to try to find something wrong with the adoption papers and get the girls sent back to China, and I knew that it was all in perfect order, so I didn't give it another thought. I'll call them off you. I'll also tell her I know what she's doing and put a stop to it. I'll tell the agency she's demented."

"Ted, you're a good man. I owe you a big thank-you."

"No, you don't. You just confirmed for me that Mom is truly around the bend. Not only dotty, but downright mean as well."

"As we're already here, I'll treat you to a burger, fries, and a drink. Just so you leave the restaurant before I do."

"It's a deal. I hate to say this, but I love fast food."

Jane watched Ted leave. The black car followed her home at a distance when she left ten minutes later.

When Jane got home, she called Shelley and said, "Take a little walk with me down the street. You'll enjoy it."

"Why?"

"You'll see," Jane said cheerfully.

Shelley joined her as they approached the black car parked down the block. Jane led Shelley to the driver's side of the car, and tapped on the window. The driver rolled down the window and said, "Who are you and what do you want?"

"You know perfectly well that I'm Jane Jeffry, and that Thelma Jeffry hired you to follow me around and report where I'd gone and with whom. As of tomorrow, you won't have this job. Thelma Jeffry has been put in a nursing home for terminal dementia. Have a good day."

"Ma'am, I just do what my boss tells me to do."

"Your boss is going to assign you to follow someone else around. Let's go home, Shelley," she said as she walked away.

When they returned to Jane's house, they were both laughing hysterically.

As Jane was pouring them cups of fresh coffee, she said, "I sneaked away to have a heart-to-heart talk with Ted Jeffry at lunch. He says he'll get rid of the detective. He thought Thelma was trying to get their baby girls sent back to China when he saw the endorsement on one of her checks. He knew she didn't stand a chance of pulling it off. Dixie won't ever let Thelma near the girls again because last time she visited Ted and Dixie, she called the girls 'Chinks.'"

"Oh no. I didn't realize how truly evil she is."

"Ted knows now. I'm sorrier for him than I am for myself. And I'm not sending her invitations to either of the weddings. I dearly hope I never have to see or speak to her again."

"I'll bet that goes for Dixie, and possibly Ted, too."

"I believe he's ready to do all he can to put her out to pasture," Jane said.

"How can he do that?" Shelley asked.

"Ted's bright and angry and loves his wife and little girls. He'll find a way."

Mel called Jane around five that afternoon and said, "I'm hungry for a Chili's burger. Want me to order pickup and bring it over? My treat."

"Oh, please do. Shelley and I were just sitting here lamenting about empty fridges."

She gave him her order, asked Shelley what she wanted, and guessed at what Todd would want.

"Why is he doing this?" Shelley asked.

"He probably has something to tell us, something we won't want to hear since he offered to pay for all three dinners."

"I'll run to the grocery store to get prepared sandwiches and microwave mac and cheese for Denise and John. Anything you want?"

"Yes, an iced angel food cake and some Ben and Jerry's Cherry Garcia ice cream. It's Mel's favorite dessert. Mine, too." Jane fished a ten-dollar bill out of her purse and handed it to Shelley.

The dining room table was set for four places by the time Shelley returned. Mel showed up at five-fifteen and they unloaded the dinners. When Todd had gone through his cheeseburger and fries, he asked if he could go back to his computer and was given permission. Mel was still on his second helping of cake and ice cream, so Jane and Shelley waited patiently to hear what he had to say.

Pushing his plate away, he said, "Jane, a bit of bad news. My mother wants my sisters to be bridesmaids. She's got her heart set on it."

Jane smiled. "No. You already told me that both your sisters eloped to escape the kind of killer bash wedding your mother would plan for them. Remember?"

Mel nodded.

"So call your sisters and ask them if they want to do that to me?"

He grinned. "I'll do it right now. I know they won't want to."

When he returned to the dining room, he said, "Done. In fact, sorted out before I even called. They are coming to the wedding, but just as guests."

"Good."

"Can we go outside and look at my office to see how it's coming along?"

"I thought you'd never ask."

The three of them went out in the backyard and walked around looking at the current status. Piles of Sheetrock were piled on big planks covered with plastic in case of rain.

Mel said, "For all my early objections, I'm really excited to see this coming together. Are you aware that there are all sorts of permits pasted to your dining room window?"

"Yes, and there have been people here who weren't

working and just seemed to be snooping. I asked the contractor about them and he said he'd called them to check that they were working to code. Vapor barriers, and such."

They were quiet for a while, simply contemplating the project.

"This is just for you two. I shouldn't even be talking about it, but I know you are both good at keeping secrets."

Shelley and Jane both propped their elbows on the patio table, leaning forward.

"First, the pathologist has determined that the heart attack came first and she might have been saved if someone had called for an ambulance quickly enough. But the cosh on the back of her neck came soon after."

"Cosh?" Shelley asked.

"A heavy blackjack. But, more interesting is that your Miss Welbourne wasn't 'technically' a 'Miss.'"

"How did the pathologist know that?" Jane asked.

"Because she had two scars from episiotomies."

Jane and Shelley both shuddered slightly. "So she'd given birth to two children?" Shelley asked.

"Yes," Mel said. "We have no idea where or who they were or where they were born, or even if both or one survived. But we will look closely into her past and try to find out."

Chapter

ELEVEN

Mel had just come into his office the next morning, when there was a knock on his door.

"Come in," he called.

It was the new officer he'd just hired the week before to take over for the one who was retiring in a month.

"Officer Needham, how can I help you?" he asked. She wasn't pretty at all. Late twenties, skinny, and pale, wore no makeup, but she'd already proved to be smart.

"I hate to bother you, sir, if you're busy."

"I haven't even started work yet. Sit down, Officer Needham, and tell me what you need."

"I don't need anything, sir. It's just that I was cruising the Internet last night and found out some things that are interesting about the name Welbourne. It's an oddly spelled name so I went searching."

"Find anything interesting?"

"Interesting, but maybe useless. There are very few people in America with that name. And I didn't find the victim's name at all. But there were lots of references to British Welbournes, even a school and a street and a couple of ancient parsons in genealogical sites. But there are even more Welbournes in Australia. I remember from a book I once read that people who went bankrupt or committed minor crimes in England in the old days were filling the jails and most of them were eventually sent off to Australia to continue to be criminals or turn their lives around."

"That is interesting," Mel said. "I never knew about this. So do you have any conclusions?"

"Sorry, sir, but I don't—I just thought it might turn out to be worthwhile to know. At the meeting yesterday you said Miss Welbourne had given birth to two children. Might it be possible to see if a person with the same name was in Chicago at the time of her death? I know it's a long shot and probably a silly one. The first place we always look for a murderer is in the family of the victim."

Mel leaned back. "Not silly at all. Why did you pause at the beginning of what you just said?"

"Because it's a very remote chance and might waste a lot of police time."

"No worry. Except I don't know if we need a warrant to ask hotels to open their reservation records or not. I'll go to legal and if it's possible, I'll send you around to the downtown hotels. Start with the best. Anyone who could afford the flight could probably afford a good hotel."

"Could you give me permission to just try it out first before you go to legal?"

"Of course. You may turn up something useful. I appreciate your input and the information you've provided."

She was prettier than he'd thought when she gave him a big smile and thanked him. A nice start to the day.

Officer Needham was back at two that afternoon. Mel's office door was open and she said, "I found some Welbournes." She was almost bouncing on her feet.

"I went to two hotels downtown and they both said they couldn't give information about guests without going to their headquarters and telling them why we need to know about certain guests.

"So I went to a third hotel, and the desk clerk was being cranky about missing his lunch break. An overweight man who must have never missed a lunch in his life."

Mel smiled back at her. "Go on, Officer Needham."

"The desk guy kept complaining that his substitute was late, and I sat down in the lobby as if I were waiting for someone, and when the substitute turned up, a spotty young man, I went back to the front desk and asked if they had records of a person or people named Welbourne staying there recently.

"He claimed he wasn't supposed to talk about visitors. He'd have to ask the man having his lunch.

"I got really chummy and friendly and said, 'Won't it be a bad idea to interrupt his lunch?'

"He grinned, glanced over his shoulder, and opened the reservation book. Turns out there were two Welbournes there during the time Miss Welbourne was attacked. They came three days before, and left two days later."

Mel said, "Sit down and tell me what else he said."

"That they were in their forties, good tippers, and had Australian passports. He said he himself had been at the front desk when they asked him to book a limo to the airport. He called the limo company and they asked him what flight number, takeoff time, and destination."

"And what was that?" Mel said, pleased that she'd gotten so much information out of a hotel employee.

"Destination was San Francisco and the man said they were staying there to see the sights before their long trip home to Sydney, to rest again, visit friends, then go home to Perth."

"This is amazing," Mel said.

"Not really. The temp at the desk liked the man. The temp was always around at lunchtime and the pair of them asked him about restaurants. The temp wasn't crazy about the man's sister, though."

"You did get first names, right?"

"William G. and Anne L."

Mel jotted the names down.

"Where can we go from here?" Officer Needham asked. She'd already gotten a bit in her mouth and was eager to pursue anything her boss wanted her to do.

"I think you need to leave that to me. I'll call some police detectives in San Francisco I've met before and ask about finding them. Apparently they stay in nice hotels. I'll tell him that a woman died on my turf and left a substantial amount of money in her will. And we're trying to find her heirs, who are seemingly staying there."

"So she left her money to them?"

Mel smiled. "Nope. She left it to various charities. Mostly shelters for abused women, and the Salvation Army. But I don't have to say that."

"How did you get the will, sir? May I know?"

"Yes, it's no secret. She lived in a luxurious condo full of antique furniture. All but the will and an old set of trust papers were in the files. But there was a key to a lockbox taped to the back of a drawer."

"But lockbox keys and paper containers have nothing about a name of the bank, sir. Just the box number."

"She'd handwritten the name of the bank on the back of the packet the key was in."

Officer Needham said, "I can understand that, sir. My grandma had a whole lot of stuff in various banks and didn't indicate what banks they were. It took my dad three years to go to each bank in Chicago. And he only found one that would allow him to use the key. The box was full of titles to cars. Most of them hadn't been owned for forty years."

Mel laughed. "That happens to a lot of people. My mother had to hire someone to open a small house safe she found behind a bookshelf in her father's house. It had the same things in it."

"May I ask another question, sir?"

"Only if you stop calling me 'sir.' It makes me feel old. And I may not know the answer."

"Yes, s—. What was the trust about?"

"It's not common knowledge, and I want you to keep it to yourself."

"I will."

"It's a trust in the name of an aunt of hers, leaving her a large amount of money to house, feed, and educate her children. I assume that given that the aunt was probably much older than Miss Welbourne, she's no longer living and the remainder of the assets have gone to Miss Welbourne's children, or have been used up."

"May I have the aunt's name and look her up on my own computer at home? There are a lot of sites that list census results, and court rulings, and such."

"So long as you only give any results to me directly."

"I wouldn't ever consider talking about this with anybody else. I promise you that. And I might not be able to find out anything."

Jane was on the phone with her new publicist. The former one had decided to become an agent.

"I'm glad to hear from you," Jane said.

The new publicist, Sandra, said, "You've received your own copies of the first book, haven't you?"

"I have. I love the cover."

"It's a good thing you and your editor and your agent all agreed to let the first two be in paperback. If the sales are good, we'll probably go to hardback for the third."

"Why is that? I'm new to this business."

"Because however charming you are at signings, most readers of mysteries don't want to invest over $24 on a new writer. But they'll pay six-fifty or even close to seven dollars to try the first two. And if they like them as well as I know they will, they'll cough up the money for the hardback for the third one."

"That makes sense," Jane said. "I feel the same way about new authors."

"Now, I've set up two chats and then signings for next week in your area. One of the mystery bookstores is downtown, one is suburban."

"Chats?"

"Just a few minutes to say a little bit about yourself. Why you took up writing, or where you grew up, or whatever you feel strongly about. Make it upbeat and smile the whole time. And then ask if anybody has questions. If they don't, the bookseller will start putting the books out for you to sign. If there are too many questions, the bookseller will know how to tactfully cut them off.

"Your driver will then take you to other major chains. She will call ahead to make sure they have the books ready for signing. Oh, sign them with a colored pen. That way readers won't think it's a machine-made signature."

Jane laughed. "I never knew there was such a thing. Any other advice?"

"Just smile all the time, no matter how tired your hand feels. I'll e-mail you the times and the names of the booksellers and the name of your escort."

"May I take someone along?"

"Do you need someone along?"

"My neighbor and best friend would like to go with me, and give me a heads-up if I quit smiling," Jane said.

"I don't see why not. And congratulations on your first book. I've read it and loved it and I understand the second one is already here. I'm going to snag a copy as soon as they copyedit it."

"Thank you for being so patient with a newbie, Sandy. I'll take all your advice."

Jane hung up and did a little dance around the living room, scaring Max and Meow, who were sleeping curled up together on the sofa.

"I'm a *real* writer now, kitties," she said, giving them both neck scritches.

Chapter

TWELVE

Jane invited Mel to come to dinner. She had a copy of her book already signed for him. "To Mel, With Love, From Jane."

She'd made crispy fried chicken breasts, mashed potatoes, and overcooked green beans with onions and bacon. Good old comfort food. After dinner she gave him the book.

"I hope you'll read it. It's really a book women will enjoy more than men. Then you never have to read another one if you don't want to."

"Jane, I intend to read every single one of them."

"Really and truly, you don't have to read them."

Quickly changing the subject, she asked, "How is your case about Miss Welbourne going?"

"Slowly. My bright new assistant has found Welbournes that may or may not be her children."

Jane asked, "Is this new assistant pretty?"

Mel laughed. "Not especially. But she's smart and dogged."

"So how did she find these people?"

Mel explained about the temp at the front desk filling in for the hungry guy who was eating lunch.

"She is clever," Jane agreed. "Do I understand that you're not sure they are related to Miss Welbourne? Granted, it's a strange name, spelled strangely."

"According to Officer Needham, there are quite a few people and places in England spelled that way. And even more in Australia."

"These people were from Australia?"

"So their passports said. And they were here in Chicago the week she was murdered."

"Where are they now?"

"They told the young man at the desk that they needed a car to take them to the airport for a particular flight to San Francisco."

"Are they there?" Jane asked.

"We don't know yet. I've put in calls to the chief of police. So far there's no sign of them. They've contacted the big expensive hotels, and have gone to the less expensive ones and even to a few bed-and-breakfast places. It's possible they're just staying with friends. Or they could have lied to the clerk at the Chicago hotel and are already back in Australia or somewhere else."

"If they're found, are you going to take DNA samples?"

"Only if they give permission. For all we know, they might be second cousins or something and they were in Chicago for some other reason. The one who claimed to be the brother might have a business with a Chicago office."

"At the same time she was murdered?"

"Anything's possible."

"But unlikely," Jane said. "There's something else you're not telling me, isn't there?"

"You're as clever as Officer Needham, aren't you?"

Jane bridled. "I certainly hope so. I wouldn't want to be outranked by your assistant."

"No chance. But she has found out a little bit about this trust thing."

"What trust thing?"

"The copy that was in Miss Welbourne's lockbox at the bank. It names a trustee for her children. No names. Just her children. The trustee was an aunt, apparently, a woman named Maud Brooker. Written in 1968."

"How was the trust funded?" Jane asked. She herself had a trust done for her own children years ago, but she had been sure to name her three children.

"By some stocks in an excavating company that must have had terrific dividends, is my guess. But my assistant can't find them. There's a mention in a newspaper in 1979 about the company merging with another company. And later that company merged with yet another."

"Excavating what?" Jane asked.

"Who knows? Digging basements for the suddenly rich Aussies? Strip mining for minerals? Nobody seems to know."

"Is the aunt still living?"

"No. Officer Needham found a death certificate for her. She died in 1989."

"Wasn't there an alternative trustee?"

"Yes, a bank in a little town that seems to have disappeared since the trust was done. It's simply a ghost town now."

"What if you never find them?"

Mel said, "It's possible that's how it will turn out. But I don't want to simply give up on this. She was murdered. These people are somewhere, and I'm determined to find them."

Jane already knew, but this reinforced her confidence that she was going to marry a very honorable man. He probably wouldn't have even liked the woman if he'd ever met her in person, but he was determined to find out who murdered her.

"Want to take a quick look at how your office is coming along?" she asked.

"I'd love to."

"I've told Mr. Edgeworth to put another door in the room going directly out into the backyard."

"Why?"

"So if you need to suddenly go somewhere, you don't need to go clear through the house and can get your car out of the garage faster."

Mel merely smiled. "I'd have never thought about that, but it is a good idea."

They went outside to stare at the semiroom. The shape of it actually looked like a real room. Even though there were no walls yet, where the doors and windows would be was obvious. So was the shape of the roof. There was even a hole for a skylight.

"Jane, in spite of my guilt about you spending all this money, I'm going to love having this room to myself." He gave her a big hug and a really good kiss.

The time passed quickly and Jane asked Shelley if she'd come along to her book signings.

"You have a driver and it seems tacky to impose on him or her. I'm not fighting the traffic to get downtown, but I'll certainly be at the second one in the suburbs."

"I guess you're right."

The driver was a woman named Barbara Smith, and very pleasant. She called Jane the day before and said, "I've called ahead to several chain stores making sure they'll have copies of your book handy for signing. I'll pick you up at nine-thirty so we can have plenty of time for the ten o'clock signing downtown, and we can grab a sandwich between there and the other store."

"I'll be ready. Is there anything specific I need to take along?"

"Just a colored pen. Anything but black. And don't

overdress. You want to look like an average person. Not a prima donna. See you tomorrow."

The first signing went really well. The bookstore was tiny and there was already a short line of people, mostly women, standing on the sidewalk outside. The bookstore owner was standing in the doorway and shook Jane's hand and thanked Barbara for being a little early. "Jane, do you need a drink before your talk?"

"Just a glass of water, please."

When she got inside, she was impressed that they had a huge poster on the wall with her picture and the cover of the book.

"How did you do that?" Jane asked.

"I didn't. Your publisher sent it last week. Stand to speak and I'll be at your side to open the book to the page you want to sign. It moves things along a lot faster."

Jane, having never done a book signing, was surprised at how considerate this was. Or simply the norm?

When the crowd outside found places around the room, the bookseller stood and introduced Jane. "She's a brand-new author. And I've read her book already and enjoyed it enormously. She has a real gift for words. We can take a few questions, then we'll get on with the signing."

The first person to put her hand up was a very young woman in dreadlocks and a big smile. "I already read your book as well. I wonder how you knew so much about the time you were writing in."

"I did a lot of research," Jane said with a grin and

added, "I didn't use anything but the most interesting things I discovered. I wanted it to be an historical mystery, not a textbook."

"Thank you, Ms. Jeffry. That's good advice. I'm writing a novel myself," she said proudly before sitting down.

"I wish you good luck," Jane said.

The second question was about Jane's background. "Have you always lived in Chicago?"

"Only after I married. My dad is a diplomat with a gift for foreign languages and my parents always took us along to the countries where he was working. That's why I've stayed where I lived in the same house for all these years."

"What's your husband think of your book?"

"My husband died in a car accident when our children were young. And I'm about to be married for the second time late this summer."

"Oh, how nice," the bookseller said. "Now we'll start the signing. I'm glad we have such a crowd. My assistant has passed out little notes so you can spell your name for Jane. Or the name of whom you're also buying a book for."

They both sat down at the table and the bookstore owner started opening the books to the title page.

Jane took a mental count of how many she'd signed and by the time she was done, she estimated she'd sold thirty-seven.

She stood back up, flexing the fingers of her right hand before shaking the bookseller's hand and thanking her.

"That's almost a record," the bookstore owner said. "All too often, authors only sell ten or twenty. We've sold out all I ordered and I will order more today. You said all the right things to interest readers."

Barbara Smith was standing at the front of the store. She also thanked the bookseller.

She opened the passenger door for Jane. "Your hand got quite a workout."

"I'm not used to handwriting anymore except to write checks," Jane said with a laugh.

They stopped at a sub shop and bought one sandwich cut in half, two bags of chips and iced tea. When they arrived at the large suburban bookstore, Shelley was waiting just outside the door.

"There's a guest inside you won't like."

"Not Thelma again?"

"No, your soon to be mother-in-law."

"Oh dear. What's she doing here? She lives in Atlanta."

"I have no idea. I just wanted to warn you."

The bookseller introduced herself and took Jane to the table at the back of the store. There was a big crowd. Jane spotted Addie in the back row and didn't flinch. Addie was reading a local real estate flyer.

Jane answered pretty much the same questions she'd been asked at the last signing. And the signing commenced pleasantly. When she left, the driver was in the car waiting in front. Jane whispered, "Lock all the doors, please."

Ms. Smith did so and looked at Jane questioningly.

Addie came outside and tapped on Jane's window. Jane rolled it halfway down and said, "Why are you here?"

"I came up to book a hotel that could serve a dinner for four hundred and supply a dance floor."

"That's not the way it works, Addie. It's my choice of sites. And why four hundred people? I don't even know two hundred people."

"We can talk about it in the car," Addie said, trying to get in the backseat and finding the door locked.

She came back to the driver's side and said, "Unlock the back doors."

"I can't do that," Barbara Smith said firmly. "I'm not insured for strangers to ride with me. I've been hired to convey Ms. Jeffry to other signings now."

And with that, she rolled up her window and drove off. In the rearview mirror Jane could see Addie holding up her fist in anger.

"Who was that woman?" the driver asked.

"To my great disappointment she's going to be my mother-in-law soon."

"Oh, my dear. I'm so sorry about that. But you stood up to her wonderfully."

Chapter

�֍

THIRTEEN

When they approached the first of the "drop-in" bookstores to sign stock, Jane asked Barbara if she could have a brief minute to speak to her future husband on her cell phone. Barbara was glad to do so. "I'll make sure they have enough copies at the front desk."

Jane called Mel. "Your mother is in town."

"What for?" He sounded alarmed.

"To find a hotel that can cater four hundred guests and host a dance after the wedding."

A long sigh from Mel. "That's none of her business. It's up to us where the wedding takes place. And even I don't know four hundred people I'd want to have there."

"Furthermore, she didn't even buy a copy of my book

at the bookstore. And she tried to break into my escort's car to talk about it more."

"Okay, I'll find her. I have her cell phone number and will stop her in her tracks. I already made it clear that this wasn't up to her. It's our choice of the place. A dance, for God's sake," he exclaimed before hanging up.

Mel called her back that evening, and said, "I've told her she can invite fifty people and we'll invite fifty or fewer. We will pick out where and when the public wedding takes place. She can cater it. She can buy whatever stuff she wants to put on the tables. You will pick out your own flowers for your bouquet and the dinner tables. But, Janey darling, her plans also included an enclosure in the invitation for where to buy gifts."

"What?" Jane yelped.

"Sorry, but it's true. We were supposed to go to Bed Bath and Beyond and pick out what we wanted in housewares, china, bedding, and crystal. Also Home Depot so I could order tools and build a deck, and buy a big monster grill."

Jane forced a bitter laugh. "No way, Mel. For one thing it's rude to do that. And we don't need anything. We're grown-up adults. I couldn't find anywhere to put any of this stuff."

"And I already have a drill with bits, and both kinds of screwdrivers. I'm not building a deck. And if we want a grill, we can pick one out ourselves."

"How about this?" she suggested. "If she insists on an enclosure, tell her we want donations to the Red Cross, the Salvation Army, and Habitat for Humanity. We'll look golden and people we don't even know will benefit from it. And we won't have to build yet another room to hold stuff we don't need or want."

"Great idea. Speaking of charities, I'm thinking about giving most of my stuff to someone. I don't want that dilapidated sofa of mine, or the complicated pasta maker, or the really scary electrical meat slicer that looks like a power saw. There's also an industrial-size Cuisinart. Do you think the Salvation Army would take it all away? They're all in their original boxes."

"Of course they could, but what on earth made you buy such silly things?" Jane asked.

"I didn't buy them. My mother sends me domestic cooking gadgets for every birthday and Christmas. I even have a monster-size breadmaker."

"How did you hide these things from her that time she came to stay with you that Christmas when your furnace went out?"

"I'd like to claim I deliberately disabled the furnace so she'd never know. But it wasn't the truth. I couldn't have done that to you, forcing her to stay at your house for the holiday. She was there for such a short time that she couldn't even look in my kitchen cabinets."

He added, "The apartment didn't even come with a fridge or stove, so I'll pay someone to haul them away as soon as she's left after the wedding. I'm sort of glad this discussion came up."

Jane almost volunteered to help him with his purging,

---

then thought better of it. It was better if he got rid of his things by himself without any input from her.

"Anyway, she's on her way back to Atlanta," Mel said. "She hates having to share her commissions with other real estate people. That's why she seldom visits me. Thank God. Anyway, we should get on with making our own plans for where this fake wedding is going to take place."

"Shelley and I will look for nice hotels that can accommodate four hundred guests. You have lots of friends and acquaintances because of your job. You can invite as many as you want. I only want my immediate family and Shelley's, and Ted and Dixie, and Uncle Jim. That's seventeen people total including Ted and Dixie's little girls. Eighteen if your mother shows up."

"You must have a lot more friends you'd like to invite," Mel said.

"Only if you include my kids' former teachers, and all of the fundamentalist church ladies Thelma knows."

"Is she coming to either of the weddings?"

"She says she'll consider both. Oh, I completely forgot to tell you what Thelma did to me."

"What was that?"

"She had a private detective following me everywhere I went. She knew exactly where Shelley and I went, what we were wearing, how long we were there."

"Good Lord! You've stopped her, I hope."

"Ted took her on. He balances her checking account and saw a check endorsed by a detective agency a couple of months ago. He thought she was investigating the adoption of their girls. He knew she'd fail to find any flaw in the paperwork, so he forgot about it until I met him in secret and told him about the forged addendum to my former husband's will."

"Worse and worse! Is she legally demented? Can't she be put away somewhere? What did she forge?"

"An addendum typed on an old typewriter I gave her—the print looked like handwriting script. It said if I remarried, the whole will was null and void. And she tried to fake his signature. Badly. Ted was already furious with her because she'd said in front of his children that they were 'Chinks.'"

Mel was so dumbfounded by this whole story that he couldn't even reply for a minute or two. "Janey, *please* don't issue an invitation to either wedding to her. She's the kind of nut case who would ruin anyone's life just with a word or two."

"There is that. But more important, Ted, Dixie, and the little girls wouldn't come to the real wedding if Thelma were coming. I want them there. I'll have to have another secret meeting with Ted so he won't tell her where and when it's taking place. And warn him to keep the fake wedding a secret as well. I can't help feeling that all those trips she took Todd on were for nothing. She really treated one of my children well. But I hope to never be in the same room with her again. I'll have to explain to Todd why she's not invited, though."

"May I come over this evening to see how the new room is coming along?" Mel asked.

"I'd love it if you did. It's almost a real room. Mr. Beckman is really moving it along as fast as he can."

Saturday morning Todd came down expecting his mother to have made him a good breakfast. But he found her sitting at the kitchen table reading a mystery novel.

"No breakfast?" Todd asked.

"Not here. I have a craving for one of those Sonic breakfast meals. Greasy, salty, with two orders of tater-tots for both of us and big cherry limeades."

She knew this would appeal to him. And she also knew if he was at his computer he wouldn't really listen to her.

They took their orders and drove to a little park near the fast-food place. When they were both so full that they needed naps, Jane said, "Todd, there's something I need to tell you about your grandmother Jeffry."

"She died?" he asked.

"No, not yet. But she's become quite dotty and mean."

"You're telling me!" he exclaimed. "I was afraid to say it."

"How did you know?" Jane was surprised that he was so perceptive about his grandmother. *She'd treated him well*, she thought. All those nice summer vacations she'd taken him along on had been fun for him.

"That last trip, remember? To Mexico?"

"Yes. Two years ago."

"It was horrible," Todd said, taking a noisy last slurp of his cherry limeade.

He went on, "She always took me to places where

there was kid stuff. Playgrounds, swimming pools, and other stuff. I liked that and she'd always take me to a zoo or a neat movie. But when we got to Mexico, she went wonky."

"In what way?"

"Lotsa ways. She wouldn't let me swim in the hotel pool for one thing. She said the staff people got to use it sometimes and the water would be dirty and maybe carry diseases. She was rude to the waiters. She thought most of them didn't understand English and would say right in front of them how lazy they were. She'd always have bottled water in her big purse to wash off the silverware before we could eat."

"Go on," Jane said.

"Well, Mom, I finally got fed up and was so embarrassed at being with her that I told her not to be so rude and mean and loud."

"How'd she take that?" Jane asked.

He took one more fruitless sip of the melting ice in his cup and said, "She said she was so disappointed in me speaking to her that way, but since you raised me, she wasn't at all surprised that I'd learned to dislike old people. I'm sorry, but you asked me."

"It explains a lot of things, Todd. First, why she never took you on another trip."

"I wouldn't have gone if she'd invited me," he said. "Not after the way she was nasty about you. It's awful to talk ugly to strangers, but worse to talk ugly about a guy's mom."

She gave him an affectionate fist thump on his shoulder. "Now it's my turn," Jane said. "She's been very nasty to me, too, recently. She hired a detective to follow me everywhere I went alone or with Mrs. Nowack. She wanted to know how we were dressed and how long we were gone, and if he could tell what we were eating or buying."

"That's horrible, Mom!"

"She's done worse things. At dinner with Uncle Ted and Aunt Dixie she called their little girls 'Chinks' and made Aunt Dixie cry all night."

" 'Chinks'? What's that mean?"

"It's a nasty word for anybody Chinese. Just like calling a black person the N word."

"I know what the N word is. In sixth grade a new girl who was black started the year in my class and a boy called her that. The teacher took him to the principal and they called his parents to take him home for the rest of the week. He never came back. I think his folks thought it was okay to say the N word and put him in another school. I see what you mean. Poor Aunt Dixie and Uncle Ted. Did Mary and Sarah understand it?"

"No. They are too young to know a word like that. And Uncle Ted and Aunt Dixie aren't ever going to let your grandmother be around them again."

"Good for them!"

"That's why Mel and I aren't inviting her to either of the wedding services. And be sure if she asks you when and where they are going to be, you must pretend you don't know or have forgotten."

"I won't. I promise. It's sorta sad. When I was a little kid, she was a nice Grandma. She isn't even a nice person anymore."

"Todd, my dear son, sometimes old ladies turn mean. If I do, promise you'll stash me away somewhere."

He put down his cup on the floor of the Jeep and turned and gave her a big hug. "You'll never turn mean. You're the nicest mom anybody could have. Could we go home now? I'm stuffed and need to figure out something about my computer."

"What's that?"

"It's going weird and doing tabs wrong. Maybe it's also turning into an icky old woman."

Both of them laughed.

Chapter

❁

FOURTEEN

Jane was once again sitting outside, in spite of the fact that every day became a little hotter as spring was getting ready to turn into full-blown summer weather. She was thinking about the talk with Todd earlier in the day. She hadn't especially wondered why Thelma hadn't taken Todd on her usual summer vacation for the last two years. If she had, she would have assumed Thelma simply thought she was getting too old to travel. Or that Todd was getting too old to go on trips with a grandmother.

No. That wouldn't play. Thelma wouldn't have thought about anyone but herself. So chalk it up to age.

All in all, it had been a good conversation and cleared up a lot of things. It allowed her to tattle to Todd about what his grandmother had said and tried to do to her in the last week without feeling guilty and whiny.

There was something else at the back of her mind that she'd been trying to grasp all day that finally emerged. It involved the next book she was writing. And the case of Miss Welbourne's death. But in reverse, so to speak.

A woman who had been in an accident and had already set up a trust for her children with a secondary trustee who was her cousin. How did she have enough money to do this, though? She had to be a widow and she'd inherited a lot of money from her deceased husband. She also had to keep her own substantial inheritance from her own parents.

The whole setup had to be convincing. How old were the children when her accident happened? How had it occurred? It was necessary for her to be in a near coma for a long enough time to justify that the cousin could take over managing the trust. And worse, how could she convince the reader that a woman could come out of a coma and remember her whole past?

Jane would have to start in her heroine's mind. Alert and intelligent as ever, but unable to speak or indicate (except from her eyes following someone in the room?) that her mind was still working.

Furthermore, her characters in her first two books, had elaborate and long names. This time she needed a down-home plain name. It couldn't be anything that started with a J, however. People who didn't know Jane well often called her Janet, or Jean, or Joyce. She didn't want readers to mix up her real name with the character's name.

Martha? No, that was her sister Marty's real name and she couldn't love and sympathize with a Martha.

Ruth? Too biblical. Sarah? Also biblical, but a nice name. How about spelling it Sara? That would work. She'd known two Sarahs along the way through the many schools she'd gone to during her childhood who were called Sally by their friends. Sally was a more "affection-ate" name. At least as far as Jane was concerned.

She hadn't brought her legal pad out to jot down notes, so she ran inside for one, refreshed her iced tea, fetched a pencil, and went back to the patio table. The workers weren't making as much noise as they had in the early stages of the room addition. There was the occasional sound of a nail gun, or a request for another roll of the insulation they were putting in between the studs. They'd also learned to leave her alone. The Porta Potty, or what-ever it was called, was on the far side of her house so none of them had to come into her house.

She supposed they thought of her as a weird writer who sat outside handwriting books. She wasn't writing a book, though. She was thinking out possibilities. Later she'd line all them up in no particular order on a file in her computer and soon begin to write the book.

She still needed a time setting. When did people begin the legal business of setting up trusts? She'd need to research that. She'd heard of trustbusters in history, long ago. The railroad barons used trusts, she suspected.

But those were big companies, not individuals. And it was probably before women could even vote. She'd let Sally settle it with a will instead.

And where would the story be set?

She found herself wanting to start the book, without worrying about chronology or legal matters. She went inside and sat down at her computer to write the first chapter.

Sally had her eyes closed and was thinking, "I've been in this bed in the hospital for a year and one week. It's good that I had the sense not to let anyone know I could hear and see. Even though that was all I could do. Thank God for Lacy."

Lacy had, after the first week that Sally was hospitalized, taken on responsibility for her. Lacy was young, tall, and strong and was the only one in the world who believed that Sally could recover. Three times every day she propped Sally up on pillows and hand fed her water and pulverized food. She'd also lift her carefully to the commode in the corner of the room when Sally needed it.

Sally would look at that part of the room as a signal to Lacy. Lacy was the only one who knew that Sally could see. And she knew, instinctively, that Sally didn't want anyone else to know. Lacy, after Maud's visit, also put a camp bed in Sally's room, so she could turn her during the night.

Lacy would bathe Sally once a day, and then gently

massage her arms and legs. What Lacy didn't know yet was that Sally was starting to feel through her fingertips and toes. Lacy's belief and care of her were working.

Sally's husband, who was also an orphan and the only child of rich parents, as was Sally, was killed on a skiing trip to Switzerland when he was buried in an avalanche. His body wasn't recovered until the spring thaw. Their children were young. Bobby was only two on his last birthday, and Amanda was four and a half. Knowing that her husband's life had been taken away too soon, she wrote a will, giving her substantial inheritance from her own parents over to her cousin Maud. Sally had no brothers or sisters and only one cousin.

Sally's inheritance from her late husband was also generous, but she held that back in the will for the welfare and education of her children. And her own welfare in the future.

During her widowhood, Sally had left the children with their nanny while Sally went to buy groceries one day, and was attacked by a purse snatcher. He'd hit her in the back with something like a pipe to knock her down. She only knew this because Lacy told her when she was sent from the hospital to the nursing home.

Her memory of Maud's first visit was still clear in her mind. Maud had come to the nursing home a month after Sally had been moved there and tried to convince the doctor that he should write up a document saying that Sally would never recover and Maud herself should have

Sally's late husband's money as well to raise Bobby and Amanda.

The doctor refused. "She's probably not ever going to recover, but she's healthy except for the spinal injury. She can swallow food and water, she can evacuate her bowels. Her heart is healthy. Her blood pressure is normal."

"But she's a vegetable and always will be," Maud claimed. "And she's stuck me with her children."

"What are you suggesting?" the doctor asked. "That we put her down like a seriously injured pet?"

"Why not?" Maud said. "She'll never be able to get out of that bed on her own. And I need more money to take care of her children."

"She'd have to make a new will for that to be done," the doctor said and then he took her arm and added, "Go away and never come back here. I'm going to see if I can find someone more honorable to take care of her children."

As it happened, after she left, he reflected that he was bound to the conditions of Sally's will as well. He couldn't place her children anywhere else any more than Maud could get her hands on Sally's late husband's money.

But after that visit, Lacy moved a camp bed into Sally's room, to make sure Maud didn't sneak back in and do harm to Sally. Lacy felt that Maud would do anything to get rid of Sally and claim not only Sally's money, but that of Sally's late husband.

On that day a month after the first year and week had

passed, Sally could feel with her fingertips, and her toes could move. A month later she looked at Lacy, and then at her own hand. Lacy did so and started to weep as she felt the strong grip of Sally's handshake. Sally made her mouth work and said in a husky whisper that was slurred, "Thank you."

Lacy wept.

Jane saved this scene to a backup disk and turned off the computer. She could go back later and make any corrections or additions to the work. She was pleased with the setup. Maud would try again and again to get all the money. Sally would gradually improve. Only Lacy would know when Sally finally took her first step by herself.

Later in the day, she checked what happened in 1903 and found very few interesting national events; she decided that the location of the hospital and nursing home should be in Virginia, near the Maryland border.

She made a brief outline of the story line, including Maud trying to kill Sally and Sally breaking Maud's nose. Lacy pretended that it was she who attacked Maud in defense of Sally when the doctor learned of the incident. Jane made sure not to give away the ending. She'd be paid part of her advance for turning in a brief outline, but she didn't want anyone to know the ending before reading the whole manuscript. Besides, Jane hadn't yet decided exactly what the ending would be. Jane, a dinosaur who still used WordPerfect instead of Word, went through what she'd written with the grammar checker, which was nutsy and priggish, and thought that more than one sentence in dialogue made the wrong parentheses. It also wanted to change every *who* to *whom*. But it was good at catching *is* for *as*, and *it's* for *its*. Fortunately Jane could ignore whatever the stupid grammar checker said.

As she was finishing up, she realized she didn't have a title for the book yet. She'd have to do a cover letter explaining this to her agent.

As she was printing, the phone rang, and Thelma said, "Jane, uu haven't ssent me an invitation to uu wedding."

Jane was taken aback by this slurred message and said, "I'm not inviting you because of what you tried to do to me."

"Uu are a bbbad gur," and there was a crashing sound.

Since the phone was still intact at Thelma's end, Jane used her fax machine in telephone mode and called Ted. "Your mother just called me and was slurring her words, and then there was a crashing noise."

"Oh God. Jane," Ted exclaimed. "Call 911, and I'll be at her house before they get there."

She did as he'd asked.

Chapter

FIFTEEN

Jane's heart was beating at a bird rate. Had her nasty remark caused the stroke or heart attack?

The answer was no. Thelma had been slurring her words even before Jane was rude to her. Still, she felt a little pity for Thelma. Jane always hoped she herself would go over like a tree when the time came. Not lingering for years of misery.

Two hours later, Ted called Jane. "My mother's had a serious stroke. She'll be in the hospital for a week, and then go into a nursing home."

"Should I visit her?"

"No. After what she's done to you and Dixie, I don't want you to go there. But I only have one week to find a good nursing home. I hate to ask you, but I know some of them are like prisons and stink of death. We need to find a good one."

"I'd be happy to help you. Tomorrow morning I have to drop something in the mail to my agent, but after that I'm free. May I bring my friend Shelley along? She'd be one more person to judge a good one."

"That's fine."

Todd had been at the kitchen table during this conversation, and asked, "Who was that?"

"Your uncle Ted. Grandmother Jeffry has had a serious stroke and he wants me and Mrs. Nowack to go with him to find a nice nursing home when she's released from the hospital."

"I'm not really surprised, Mom. She was always mad at somebody. She was getting worse and worse about everything."

Jane was glad Todd was so down-to-earth about this.

"Want me to call Mike and Katie again?"

"If you want to, please do."

Ted picked up Jane and Shelley at nine-thirty. He had a list of five nursing homes. The first one was horrible. There was a big room filled with people in wheelchairs, grouped so they could watch television in the large room. The floors hadn't been cleaned. The room stank of urine overlaid with the scent of a disgusting air freshener.

Shelley asked to be shown some of the rooms. Each had two beds with a curtain between them. The sheets were rough and didn't smell clean.

This place was universally voted unacceptable.

The next was even worse. It looked like a jail facility. Blank white walls. Side tables bolted to the beds. No common room at all. Each room had a bathroom without handicapped bars in the shower.

The third place was marginally acceptable. Clean, but plain. There was an empty room they were invited to see. White walls, clean white floors. It didn't smell bad. The sheets were soft and clean and neatly made. But there was no sense of home to it. They hadn't seen a single nurse or attendant in the hallway.

The fourth one was stunningly elegant. It looked like a fine hotel. Pictures on the walls. A television in every room. A few even had two rooms, a sitting room, a bedroom, and a sparkling clean bath with all that a handicapped person would need. There was a nice restaurant for those who were ambulatory. There were white tablecloths and napkins and fresh flowers on each table, which seated four in comfort. Room to get close to the table in a wheelchair. There wasn't a carpet, but the tile floor was lovely.

Ted, Jane, and Shelley met with the manager. A woman wearing a good light gray suit, a white silk shirt, and restrained jewelry. Ted introduced Jane and her friend Shelley.

The manager said that they did have one room available now. The cost was rather high, but Ted didn't care and it was the closest nursing home to his own house.

She asked about the patient's condition and was told it was a serious stroke. Ted added, with perfect honesty, that she was a difficult person. Not friendly at all.

"We are equipped to deal with women like that," the manager said with a smile. "She'll have her meals delivered to her room and a young woman to help feed her soft, nourishing food, and clean her up if she spills things on herself. Will she have visitors?"

"Only me. She's been cruel to my sister-in-law, Jane, and very nasty to my wife. My mother will probably be visited by some of the ladies from her church."

"Have you been to other nursing homes?" the manager asked.

"Three of them. All unacceptable. We had a fifth to look at, but this is the right one."

Jane and Shelley left the room while Ted was signing a contract and putting a down payment on the room.

"You made the right choice," Jane said as he was driving her and Shelley home. "And you were brutally honest about how difficult she'll be."

"Thanks, Jane. At least she's pretty much out of everybody's way, except for me and the church ladies. I'll make sure that they are not around there when I'm visiting."

When Jane and Shelley came home, and were having coffee, Shelley said, "I don't think I've ever met Ted before.

Jill Churchill

I've seen him and his wife and girls when he comes to visit you. He's a very nice man."

"And a sensible one, too. It was a good idea to take two women along. If one of them had been Dixie, she'd have opted for the worst place we saw, and I wouldn't blame her. I think that without Thelma hanging out at the main office and interfering in the business, Ted will be much happier and more productive. I probably should send her flowers when she's moved in there."

"It would just make her mad to have a gift from you, Jane."

"It would please the staff who have to wait on her though. Speaking of flowers, I've insisted to Mel and his mother that I choose my own bouquet. I wouldn't trust Addie to pick one out. It would probably be a big pot of cactus plants. Is the plural of that cacti?"

"So where do you want to shop for something you'd like?"

"This is probably silly," Jane said, "but I noticed a florist shop across the street from the community center where we took those classes. The window was full of lovely arrangements."

"I noticed that, too. By the way, have you asked Mel if Miss Welbourne left any notes for the last session?"

Jane made a head-slapping motion. "I'm sorry. I simply forgot about that what with so many other things going on. Willard, the room addition, Addie's visit, and working on my next book. I'll ask him the next time I hear from him. I promise."

Mel called Jane that evening, apologizing for not being in touch for the last few days. "This Welbourne case is driving me nuts."

"What's happening?"

"Nothing. I've wired the authorities in Perth, Australia. There is a house there owned by the people we're looking for. But nobody is there. Only a neighbor lady who comes in daily to feed the cat, clean the litter box, and give the cat a fresh bowl of water. The neighbor is mad. She's never heard from them since they left. She hasn't had a postcard, letter, or phone call saying when they'd be home. She's doing this for free and doesn't even like the people or the cat."

"You left a message with someone, I assume?"

After a moment of irritated silence, Mel said, "Of course I did."

"Sorry. I've had a few bad days as well. But before I tell you about them, I'd promised Shelley I'd ask you a favor," Jane said.

"What kind of favor?" he snapped.

"Mel, remember that we're engaged," she said as sweetly as she could.

"Sorry. I didn't mean to be so rude, Janey. I'll be happy to do Shelley a favor if I can. What is it?"

"She's curious about the missing lesson we were to take about safety. If you found the notes she'd prepared for that meeting, we'd like to see what we missed. Unless, of course, they are some kind of evidence."

"I do have some notes. They're sort of haphazard, and

seemingly not related to the murder. I have to keep them, anyway, but I could fax you a copy. Now, what's happened in the last few days to you?"

"Thelma Jeffry apparently had a small stroke and called me to berate me for not sending her invitations to both weddings. She was already slurring her words. Then when I started to reply, I heard a crashing noise and had to call Ted and 911 on my fax machine. She must have had a second stroke, worse than the first. She's still unconscious in a hospital and Ted wanted help choosing a nursing home. Shelley and I went along with him. I guess for a woman's take on where she'd want to be if she ever wakes up."

Mel said, "I should say I'm sorry about this, but I'm not. I've met her a few times and found her intolerable."

"That's the general consensus," Jane replied.

"Did she leave a will?" Mel asked.

"I haven't had the nerve yet to ask Ted. I assume her third of the profits will be used for the expensive nursing home. But she did have wills in mind recently. She might have left her third portion of the profits of the pharmacy chain to her church. Which wouldn't be fair to Ted. He should inherit her third when she eventually dies."

"That's going to be tricky, isn't it?"

"There's time enough to ask Ted later. Ted is the head of the accounting department and also does Thelma's books and balances her checkbook. If she'd recently written a big check to an attorney to make a new will, he'd know about it. It's really none of my business."

"Janey, at least she's unlikely to come to either wedding to make a scene."

"True," Jane admitted. "Come see your office progress this evening if you can get away."

"I'd be glad to. I'm at a dead stop on this case right now. Maybe a nice evening will encourage me enough to try something new."

Chapter

SIXTEEN

Jane had made her favorite summer pasta salad. Little elbow pasta cooked in chicken broth, white chicken meat cut into small squares and browned slightly. Then minced onions, finely sliced celery, mayo mixed with a hint of nutmeg and a mere breath of curry powder. Nobody had ever guessed there was curry powder in it, but everyone asked what the mystery ingredient was that made it so special. With this she served toasted rounds of bread with Brie spread on it. And a good beer or lemonade depending on who wanted what.

Mel always chose a cold Coors. The real Coors, not the Light Coors. Todd chose the lemonade. And ate most of the toast and Brie.

When he'd returned to his room and computer, Jane

took Mel through the dining room and opened the door to his own office. It wasn't an office quite yet. But most of the main parts were done. Some of the studs already had insulation installed. The tiny bathroom had a sink and toilet, ready to install but no door or flooring yet. All but one of the windows were in place, the one which had arrived damaged and was on back order. The empty space was sealed with plastic sheets to keep birds, bugs, and dirt out.

Mel was impressed. "This might be done by the time we're married."

"That's what Mr. Edgeworth expects. He's here almost every day. I hear the general contractor groan quietly every time he shows up. Mel, I've been thinking about this case you're on with Miss Welbourne's death. I have an idea."

"What is it?" he asked eagerly.

"Involve the journalists here and in Australia."

"How?"

"You should be able to get copies of their passport photos from the passport part of the government if you explain why you need them."

Mel laughed. "Just like that? I ask nicely? And they give me what I want? Jane, have you ever dealt with a federal government agency?"

"Not really. Just the IRS."

"Okay, Janey, suppose I can get a copy of their passports? What then?"

"You pay to have the pictures reproduced in something like the Sunday magazine supplement to the *New York*

Times. **People all over the country take that. And there must be the equivalent sort of paper in Australia."

"So how do they respond to the ad?"

Jane said, "Oh, I hadn't thought about that. What about a 1-800-something number."

"And pay thousands of people to answer the phones twenty-four hours a day? And deal with the loonies who think there's something in it for them to pretend they know something? 'I saw a couple that looked like that last week in a bar in Denver,' or 'I once met a couple in La Jolla that looked just like them two years ago. I think their names were something like Well-something,' Or even nut cases who want to pretend they are one of them."

"Okay, it was an idea. You said you'd hit a brick wall of sorts trying to find them. This could be the way."

She knew she hadn't planned this out well enough before presenting it. And it wouldn't be done. She really wanted to help him though. It was fine for his brilliant assistant to find out the whole history of Australian Welbournes, but it hadn't resulted in anything.

She should have stayed out of it.

But Mel was aimlessly thinking about Jane's suggestion when he arrived at his office the next morning. Maybe some variation of Jane's idea might work. Find a few rabid go-getter journalists in America and Australia to print the pictures and take it from there. If he'd even mentioned the police budget covering dozens, if not more, people to answer phones, he'd be drummed out of his job.

He turned the first stage of this over to Officer Needham. "Would you burrow through the Internet and find out a couple more things for me?"

"I'd be glad to." She sat down and opened her notebook and took a pencil out of her pocket. "Shoot."

"I need, first, to know who is the most rabid, hardworking reporter on the *New York Times,* and get me his or her telephone number. Or just his extension number there."

"And next?" she asked.

"Find out if Australia has a newspaper that's more or less equivalent to the *New York Times.* Read all over the country, like the Sunday edition of the *New York Times.*"

"And then?" She had the feeling there was more to this.

"A copy of the passports for the Welbourne brother and sister. Maybe the hotel where they stayed made a color copy of them. Even if it's black-and-white, we need it."

Officer Needham rose. "Is that all?"

"It's plenty, isn't it?"

"No. I think it will be fairly easy. I'll have to catch the lunch temp at the hotel again. And I'll make a point of wearing lipstick and eye shadow this time."

She almost bounced out of the room.

She was back three hours later. "It cost me a double

chocolate muffin to get a color copy for the lunch replacement. Told him to hide it in his locker so his boss wouldn't smell it lurking somewhere nearby. But I have it. I've also made a list of *New York Times* reporters. I had to pay by credit card to read their columns. But I found two possibilities. I've written them down. I also found a good reporter in Sydney, Australia."

She presented the paperwork. She'd made copies of the pieces she'd read by the reporters.

"You'll be reimbursed for the cost. Fill out the form and I'll countersign it. You've done a good job," Mel told her.

When she'd filled it out and gone, he sat reading what she'd found. And called to make an appointment with his immediate superior to go over the plan and get an authorization to send the copy of the passport pictures to the New York and Australian newspapers.

"Are you planning to give the names on the passports?" his superior, John Whitmore, asked.

"Only to the reporters. They'll be asked not to give the names out, and barely hint at a legacy. Not that her children are getting anything from her estate, but there will be loonies who want to try anything for a little cash and pretend they are the people on the passport pictures."

"Good idea, but how do the reporters weed them out?" Whitmore asked.

"By requiring them to spell out their mother's full name."

"Is it a strange name?"

"Elinor Brooker Welbourne," Mel replied, writing it out in capital letters for the file.

He got approval for the plan and Officer Needham's expenses. The man who was in the chain of authority ranking right above Whitman had been nagging Mel for months to take over when Whitman retired at the end of the summer. Mel hadn't agreed and hadn't told him why. It was because it was purely a desk job like today's.

Whitman hadn't left his office for decades to be on the scene of a crime. He never met the suspects or witnesses to get an impression of how truthful they were being. Not that Whitman didn't do his job well. He looked over every single report in detail and had a good memory for following up on the results. But he had grown fat and clumsy. Mel didn't want to run to fat, sitting at a desk all day long.

The part of the job Mel enjoyed most was the first-hand view of the crime scene, the people—the good ones and the bad ones—that he met along the line of each crime he investigated.

While Mel was making his calls to the two reporters, Jane and Shelley were at the scene of the murder of Miss Welbourne.

Before they got to the scene Jane had stopped at the bank for a whole roll of quarters. She put quarters in the parking meter until it refused to take another coin. Neither of them planned to be there for eight hours, but it would be a boon to some other driver to find so much free time available.

They stopped by the community center and read the schedule for the day. There was a class in swing dancing, and a book club meeting, and a bus in front to take mothers and their small children to the nearest library from ten to noon.

Jane and Shelley went across the street to the florist shop and sighed with pleasure at the cool humid fragrant atmosphere inside.

"I'm Jim Torrady, the owner. Anything special you ladies need? Or just looking around, which you're welcome to do."

"It smells wonderful in here," Jane said. "I'm getting married in six weeks and I want to order bouquets for myself and for my matron of honor," she said, indicating Shelley.

"Do you want something fragrant?"

"By all means. Do you have gardenias?"

"Of course. They smell wonderful."

Jane said, "Now this is going to sound silly but there will be a civil wedding the day before the big one. Can I use the gardenias for two days or are they too perishable?"

"They last fine. Just put them in a big plastic bag with a slightly damp paper towel and keep them in the refrigerator overnight."

"That sounds wonderful."

"What else do you want in the arrangement?"

"What do you suggest? I don't want it to be huge, and I'm wearing an emerald green suit, not a white dress."

"Small leaves of green and white ivy would be my suggestion. And ivory-colored ribbons to grab to throw it."

"Now, Shelley, what kinds of flowers do you want to carry yourself?"

"Do I have to? I don't even know what I'm wearing. We've wasted a lot of time fretting over what you were going to wear."

"That's true. We *do* have to sort that out soon. We have plenty of time to come back again. I'll bring along another roll of quarters."

"A roll of quarters?" the florist asked.

"Last time I was on the block I didn't notice the parking meters and I was heavily fined. I put in all the quarters the meter would accept this time."

Jim Torrady laughed out loud.

So did Jane. She said to Shelley, "I have a yearning to wear a little hat. I wonder if there are still hat stores."

Mr. Torrady said, "There's one right around the block; it backs up to this shop. She has a good selection. My wife loves any occasion to wear hats and she always buys them there."

"Let's go look, Shelley. We have seven more hours on the parking meter."

Shelley came along willingly. "I'd love to wear a little hat, too."

The shop that backed up to the florist's had dozens and dozens of hats displayed and almost all of them were pretty.

"Welcome, ladies, I'm Madelyn the Hat Lady. How can I help you?"

"I'm Jane Jeffry and this is my matron of honor. I'm getting remarried in six weeks and I want a little hat to wear. Sort of a beret, off center."

"I have those. Let me bring a few to you to consider." She picked out four and Jane tried them on in a three-sided mirror that showed how the hats looked from every angle. The first one was too big. The second too small. The third one was red.

The red one was the perfect size and sat well on her head with a few bobby pins built-in to hold the hat in place.

"That's the wrong color, but it would look great if it was the same as your dress," Shelley said. "Let me try it on, too."

They gushed in unison. "We'll be back with what we're wearing so you can make a color match. Can you do that, Madelyn?"

"Of course I can. How about coming back the first of next week with the dresses so I can find a perfect match."

"Done. Shelley, remind me to bring the quarters."

"Quarters?"

Jane explained about the fine for the parking meter.

"Aren't they obnoxious? I have a parking space behind my shop that doesn't have a meter, but I always remind customers to feed the meters and keep lots of quarters in a jar for them. See you on Monday or Tuesday. Wednesday is when I take off the afternoon to shop for fabrics and threads and netting."

"We'll be back Tuesday at the latest."

They both left the shop happy and Jane suggested they stop by the community center and watch the people dance for a few minutes.

There were five couples and it was practice not lessons. All of them were skilled. The young women wore short circular skirts under which they wore colorful bloomers. And the young men had sort of slouchy tuxes so they could move around well.

Jane and Shelley found it fascinating. "I've never seen dancing like that," Shelley said, as one young man threw his partner over his shoulder and back between his feet.

"Sure you have. It was a rave in the forties musical movies."

One of the other young men turned his partner in a cartwheel but his hands must have been sweaty and he lost his grip. She fell on the floor and jumped right back up. He rubbed his hands on his trousers and they tried it again, her turquoise bloomers flashing as she spun.

"That would have at least broken my arm," Shelley said. "I can't take anymore. Let's go shopping at the mall for a dress for me. I'd prefer black, like the men are wearing, if you don't care."

"Perfect. I'll stand out like a big green parrot," Jane said with a laugh.

Chapter

✾

SEVENTEEN

Jane had driven them today. She knew her cautious driving drove Shelley crazy, just as Shelley's driving scared Jane to death. When they got back to Jane's Jeep, there wasn't a car parked behind them, so Jane could back up a little to pull out into the street. As she did so, she stopped.

"Why are we just sitting here?" Shelley asked.

"There is no traffic behind me except a small red car pulling into where I was parked. I want to watch him as he goes to the parking meter."

Sure enough, the man got out with presumably a couple of quarters in his hand, looked at the meter, and then at Jane's Jeep. He approached the car and Jane rolled the window down.

"Are you the one who almost filled that meter up?"

"I am."

"That was generous. I've gotten two parking tickets here. It's a regular stop I have to make once a week. I'll do the same favor for someone else," he said with a smile.

"Sort of like borrowing a cigarette from a stranger, knowing you'll do the same thing for some other stranger someday. It evens out," Jane said.

"Exactly. Thanks again," he said, departing on his errand.

Jane drove off smiling.

Shelley said, "That was a nice man. And you are a nice woman. In spite of driving at a turtle's pace."

While Jane was driving them home, in her own sedate way to protect her Jeep, she said, "If you want to wear black, why not try on that black skirt and jacket I bought. We're about the same size, and you don't have to buy something new."

"I'd love buying something new," Shelley said, "but if it fits me, I'll take you up on the offer. Saves me a trip to the mall and trying on lots of clothes I'm not crazy about."

The long black skirt and short, fitted jacket looked just as good, if not better, on Shelley than it had on Jane.

"We'll share it," Jane said. "What sort of blouse are you going to wear?"

"A gardenia-colored silk chemise," Shelley said.

As she was taking the outfit off, the phone rang.

It was Ted Jeffry. "Jane, Mother has just been moved to the nursing home. I know you wanted to send flowers to the staff. Here is the address."

"Wait a sec. I won't remember it if I don't write it down in my address book."

He gave her the address and added, "It's Suite 315. I know you said you wanted to send flowers to the staff that's forced to take care of her."

"I just found a wonderful florist. He's making my bridal flowers. I'll call him right now. He gave me his card. And I'll keep sending arrangements every two weeks until—well, until she is gone." Jane didn't want to say "dead." Not that she thought it would have deeply offended him.

"I'll visit again tomorrow late in the day and report on the flowers," Ted said.

While Shelley was putting her clothes back on, she asked once again if Jane had remembered to ask Mel if they could see a copy of the notes Miss Welbourne had made for the last meeting they'd expected to attend.

Jane slapped her head. "I think I asked him. And he probably forgot." She paused for a moment. "On the other hand, maybe I forgot to ask. I'll call him right after I call the florist."

The florist they'd visited had given Jane his business card, so she rang him up to place the order.

"My mother-in-law has had a stroke and been moved from the hospital to a nursing home and I want to send flowers to the nursing home."

"What sort of flowers do you want?"

"I was thinking of fragrant lilies just coming into bud, and the same with roses. A bit of ferns, perhaps, to fill in."

"I can do that today. What is the address and her name?"

Jane gave him the address and the suite number of the nursing home, added that she wanted the delivery to be to the staff taking care of her.

"That's a bit odd, Ms. Jeffry."

"Not really. She's a nasty woman, and a full-fledged bigot. The people who will have to take care of her won't enjoy doing so."

"I understand. My late mother-in-law was the same sort of woman. I'll have the flowers delivered today."

"Let's make it an every two weeks renewal until she's no longer alive. Are you ready to take down my credit card number?"

Her next call was to Mel. "Did I remember to ask you if you could share Miss Welbourne's notes about the next meeting with Shelley and me?"

"You did ask, and I forgot. Want me to fax them to you right now?"

Jane and Shelley read through the notes and found them fascinating. The theme was American Flying Tips. She said first, don't buy a black suitcase. Ninety percent of bags coming off a plane were black. Buy a brown or red or bright blue bag and make a pompom.

You could buy a pompom kit at a craft store with instructions. If you can't find one, find something the size of a paperback book.

Leave several long strings of yarn along the top of

the book, then wrap very lightly about forty times. Then pull the ends of yarn tight, and cut through the whole back half of wound yarn. Pull the yarns more tightly and double knot around the wad of yarn. Secure the pompom's long strings to the handle. Use bright colors of yarn; mix colors if you want to.

The next travel hints weren't about safety, but practical suggestions. Take ordinary wire, or better, plastic hangers, in a side pocket of the suitcase. Most hotels have hangers too small to hang over the shower rod, preventing you from hanging something wrinkled over the rod and running hot water to shake out the wrinkles.

If you have clothing along prone to wrinkling, wrap it lightly in plastic covers from the dry cleaners.

Then she went on to describe locking the suitcase. Get a couple locks with all the keys in the package the same. Every good hardware store has these. But don't lock the bag if you're checking it through. It's likely that if the airline wants to search your bag that they'll break the lock. Carry extra locks and keys inside the bag or in your carry-on or purse. That way if you leave your bag in a hotel room, you can lock the bag every time you leave the room. Cleaning staff aren't all honest people.

Before you go through the security gates, take off your shoes and use Purell on your feet and inside your shoes. Many people are going barefoot and some of them have athlete's foot. It's highly infectious. If you're checking through your luggage, put the bottle back inside it. You can't carry on gels. If you're not checking baggage, buy a very small bottle of Purell and throw it away and buy another little bottle for your return trip.

Put your ID and boarding pass in your front pocket, so they are easy to show at check-in (if you are checking any luggage) and later when you go through the security gates. The rest of the trip, keep your schedule in your locked suitcase at the hotel.

If you feel you absolutely must take along a laptop computer, save all your e-mail and your tax information on discs. Homeland Security might seize the laptop to examine whom you've been e-mailing, how much money you make, business relationships. This should be illegal, but don't take the risk if you don't have to.

Also find a small local phone company instead of the big ones who are sharing information about whom you've called and who has called you. Almost every large city has a small local telephone exchange. Make sure your phone produces digital signals. And be aware that anybody can listen to what you're saying on a cell phone.

"I wish Miss Welbourne had lived to tell us this. It's all useful, practical information," Shelley said.

"I had no idea that people could listen to you talk on a cell phone," Jane remarked.

"I think I've heard that before. All you need is a certain kind of listening device. I can't think off the top of my head what it's called."

"I'll be sure that my phones are all digital, whatever that means. And I'll be careful what I say on my cell phone from now on."

*   *   *

While Shelley and Jane were talking this over, Mel was on the phone with the Australian reporter.

"Say, mate, how am I to cope with all the loonies who call to report having seen these people, or claim to be one of them?"

"Easy," Mel said. "Here are the relevant dates they were in Chicago. So dismiss anybody who saw them earlier. As for those people stupid enough to try to claim that they are one of the people who are being looked for, make them spell out the name of their mother exactly. I'll spell it out for you. It's an unusual spelling. And you are welcome to hint carefully about a large estate. Even though it's not being left to them. But if you hear from someone who has seen or heard where they are since the date they left Chicago, question them, and if you think they are telling the truth, let me know."

"You're a canny bloke, I gotta admit. This is going to be a bit of fun after all. Give me your number so I can report back to you if the right one turns up."

Mel did so, and hung up smiling, then called the reporter from the *New York Times* and repeated all the same information. That reporter responded as positively as the Australian reporter. Mel gave him his phone number.

"I already have it. I saw it on the caller ID. I'll get back to you as soon as I can if I get a result."

Chapter EIGHTEEN

Time seemed to Jane to be racing along. She heard from her mother via e-mail, that the Danes and Americans had worked things out earlier than expected and they could be in Chicago in three weeks. Instead of six weeks.

There was suddenly a rush to make firm plans. She called three or four hotels to make reservations to walk through the set up for wedding, food, and a dance floor for four hundred guests at most.

Two of them were already too booked up. So she called another two and they agreed to meet her this week.

She called Shelley to ask her to come along to look at hotels.

"Why not just go with the one Paul owns along with

several other investors? The one where the mystery conference was held."

"Duh! Why didn't I think of that first? Of course."

"They can be trusted to keep tabs on Addie. Keep the guest list down to four hundred and if she tries to add additional bridesmaids and groomsmen, they'll seat them in the audience, instead of with the wedding party."

"Let's go over now and set this up."

Shelley unearthed the correct planner for this meeting and they were both glad to know she immediately recognized how important the name Nowack was.

Jane explained that her future mother-in-law was a bulldozer, and wanted to do the wedding. "She wants to invite four hundred of her best friends and stuff in a lot of extra people as bridesmaids and groomsmen. You'll have to work with her and keep it to four hundred and no extra people at the front of the ceremony. Can you do that?"

Miss Tarlington's eyes went wide with pleasure. "I can and will. I've dealt with women like this before and know how to keep them in their proper places. In fact, your timing is excellent. We were fully booked up for other weddings until yesterday when the bride changed her mind. Her plan was for three hundred guests. I'll have to check this to make sure we can use the same space, however, for four hundred."

Shelley interrupted.

"Jane, think about this: These people Addie wants to invite are clients, not personal friends or family. They might be grateful to her for getting them a good price for a house they wanted. But that's all. First, not one of them has probably ever met Mel in person. And forgive me for saying this, but they've probably never *heard* of you, either. Second, maybe some of them don't even like her because the plumbing on the second floor flooded the living room the day they moved in, or the hot water tank blew up the next week because she hired a bad inspector."

Shelley went on, "Why would any of them want to come to a wedding for Mel, whom most of them have never even met? Why would clients of hers endure the horror of the Atlanta airport, paying for tickets, an expensive hotel for the sake of one free meal when they're here? Wouldn't it be easier for them to just contribute to one of the charities you've listed instead of wedding gifts?"

Miss Tarlington was grinning. "Given what you've just said, Mrs. Nowack, I'd bet at least seventy-five or even a hundred won't show up? We don't like wasting good food on no-shows. I'll make a point of contacting her every couple days to learn her numbers of responses. How many guests have you invited, Ms. Jeffry?"

"Forty-five at the very most, including my family, my new husband's best friends in the police department and their spouses, if they have one."

"That's great. I'll be in touch with you about regrets as well."

Jane said, "Mrs. Nowack is right. We really might be lucky." And then went on to say, "The groom's mother is allowed to determine the catering, since she's paying for it. She can't determine the flowers. I'm dealing with that myself."

"I'll make a note about this."

"Do I need to make a down payment on the rental of the space?"

"No. You're a friend of Mrs. Nowack. Let the future mother-in-law do that. Give me the date so I can reserve the right room. Will you be booking rooms for your own guests?"

"Just my mother, dad, and the best man. Plus me and my new husband."

"What about me?" Shelley asked.

"You and Paul have a suite that you need to reserve today."

"I'll do that right now," Miss Tarlington said.

When they got home, Jane called Addie. She had her office number and her cell phone number, but Addie had never given Jane her home number. Mel knew it, of course, and there was no way she would ask for it.

Addie wasn't at her office, so Jane called the cell phone number. Addie picked up. "Addie VanDyne. Who is this?"

"Jane."

"Jane who?"

Jane gritted her teeth and said, "Jane Jeffry."

"What do you need?"

"It's something *you* need to know. The timing of the wedding has been moved up by three weeks."

"That's unacceptable."

"Does that mean you're not coming for either wedding?" Jane asked, hoping desperately for Addie to say yes.

"I'll talk to you later. I have a client in my car."

The client was obviously more important than Jane and even her only son.

Jane hung up and went outside to smoke one cigarette. She had only two left in the pack she'd bought two weeks ago. The way things were going, she feared she'd soon be buying them by the carton.

Jane hadn't even been able to tell Mel yet about the date changing. She'd left several messages for him earlier and been told his line had been in use for quite a long time.

"It's not vital," Jane said. "Just ask him to call Jane when he's free."

He finally called two hours later. "I've taken some of your advice and contacted the press to help find Miss Welbourne's children, if in fact they really are her children."

"Is there any doubt of that?"

"Not much. But anything's possible. Sorry I had the phone line tied up so long. What's up?"

"The date of the wedding has been moved to three weeks earlier. My dad worked things out in Denmark quicker than he thought it would take."

"The sooner the better," he replied. Jane could tell from the tone of his voice that he was smiling.

"You need to talk to your mother about this."

"Haven't you told her yet?"

She hated to rat on Addie. After all, he was her only son, and he might actually care what she thought. Mel knew his mother's flaws, but in spite of them, she'd produced and raised a very good man.

"I tried," Jane said. "But she was riding around with a client and said she'd get back to me later. I've also booked rooms for the fake wedding at that hotel where the mystery conference was. You, me, Shelley and Paul, and my parents and Uncle Jim will be staying there, too. I don't know if your mother wants to book one as well. You might want to ask her. She also needs to confirm to a Miss Tarlington to make a down payment to hold the room for the wedding and the dinner and dancing. Here is the telephone number."

When he'd written it down, she could hear in the background, "Some reporter is waiting on line two."

Jane said, "I'll let you hang up and answer that. Call me back after you talk to your mother."

She'll blame it on me, Jane thought. *And I hope he'll object.*

At least it was a good reason to get back to planning her book about Sally. Shelley had found the right hotel. And the right person to work with there, who could cope with Addie without involving herself. All she had to do was wait for her hat to be made, give the new dates to the florist, and look forward to spending time with her parents. She'd been in touch with them through e-mail and phone calls, but hadn't seen and visited with them at leisure for several years.

"Shelley, I need to call Katie and Mike to let them know the changed date. Then we have to go to the hat shop with my dress."

Katie was upset. "Mom, this is on a Friday and Saturday, right? I can't be gone long. Could you get me a plane ticket for early Thursday morning and another early one on Monday morning? I really wanted to spend time with Grump and Nana."

"I've booked them in a suite at the hotel. They don't need the second bedroom. You can stay there. And I'll tell you the flight and send a car service for you both ways."

"Thanks, Mom. That'll be perfect."

Mike didn't care. "It's only a short drive from here. I hadn't even told my boss when I'd be gone. So any time suits me."

When she'd booked the flight for Katie and made a copy of both sides of the credit card to send along for the e-ticket, and when she'd dropped it off at the FedEx box at the corner of the block, she called Shelley. "I have all the travel plans lined up. Let's take my emerald suit to the hatmaker."

Jane had the rest of the roll of quarters along and fed them into the parking meter and then went back to the shop.

"Here's the suit I'm wearing," she told Madelyn. "I

hope you can match the color. And we're shorter on time than I thought. The wedding is only three weeks from now, instead of six weeks."

The milliner held up the dress and said, "I think I already have a good match. I'll hunt through the greens and we'll take a look."

She returned ten minutes later with a length of perfectly matching matte silk fabric. "I usually use this as liner but I'll line it with something a little sturdier."

"How do I make sure it doesn't slip right off my head?" Jane asked

The milliner picked up another beret and turned it inside out. "There are three little combs that hold it. Let me show you right now how to use them."

She put Jane in front of the three-way mirrors and showed her how to adjust the combs so they wouldn't slip, or make her hair look odd.

Next Shelley tried out the black one she'd chosen. She looked fabulous in it.

"I can have this green one done by the end of the week," she said.

"I'll be back on Friday then," Jane said. "What time do you open?"

"At nine, but wait until ten or you'll never get a parking place. There are so many deliveries to shops around here that you'd have to park blocks away."

This time Shelley had driven and refused to wait to see if someone pulled into the place they'd vacated and the meter showed another five hours.

"When we pick up my hat and dress, we're almost done."

"Except for dealing with Addie. Didn't she say she'd get back to you about the dates?"

"I'm keeping a close eye on the caller ID. Mel is going to have to deal with her from here on out."

"But will he?"

"He's been coping with her bossiness all his life. He must know by now how to control her."

Chapter

❀

NINETEEN

With almost everything Jane needed to do for the weddings done, she was eager to get back to Sally's story. She wasn't going to actually write another scene until she'd made her list of twenty or thirty things that might or might not happen in the story. She enjoyed this process. They were in no particular order, and could be deleted or added to whenever she thought up something new.

This had been suggested to her at the mystery conference she and Shelley had attended. A well-known writer who had befriended Jane had mentioned it. "That way you never sit down at the computer and say to yourself, 'Where on earth do I go in the next chapter? You have many choices.'"

Jane, following this excellent idea, sat down to think and make notes. In no time at all, she had thirteen good suggestions of scenes and clues, and characterizations. She'd think about them and add more later as her mind threw out new plot twists.

One important scene was calling out to her though.

Maud comes back, walks into Sally's room, and tries to smother Sally with a pillow. Maud doesn't even notice that Sally's eyes are open. Sally swings her right arm and smacks Maud right in the nose. Maud screams. Lacy, who is napping on the cot, tosses away the pillow and grabs a towel, and rubs the blood off of Sally's hand. And a good thing that she does. A moment later, the doctor arrives for his routine afternoon visit, bursting into the room.

"What's going on here?"

Maud, her fingers bloody, pinching her nose shut, is screaming and pointing at Sally. "That woman hit me! She's broken my nose."

The doctor hands Maud a small towel and says, "You foolish woman. Sally can't even move her fingers. You're making this up."

"I did it," Lacy says. "I saw her trying to smother Sally and I ran around the bed and hit her in the nose."

The doctor looks at Lacy and asks, "Why don't you have blood on your hand then?"

"Because I wiped it off," Lacy says, showing him the towel.

Jane could hardly wait to write and expand this scene. But she didn't want to write it now. She'd just jot it down and save it for later. It would have to be more dramatic after she'd brooded over it.

Meanwhile, she reverted to her chronology book. She liked to make the story brisk and not take months or years. She paper-clipped the notes in order and put them in her filing drawer with her other research.

While she was doing this, the phone rang. She recognized Addie's cell phone number and just let it ring. When it quit, she called up the stairway to Todd, "If the phone rings again, don't answer it."

"Why not?"

"Because it's Mel's mother, trying to harass me about her extravagant ideas for the wedding. I want Mel to calm her down before I speak to her."

"Good on you, Mom," he said in what he thought was a cockney accent and wasn't convincing.

The phone did ring again. And one more time. This time Addie left a message. "Jane, where are you? I've already called three times. Call me back immediately."

"Immediately? I left a phone message for her yesterday," she said as Todd came back down the stairs.

"What's for lunch?" he asked.

"Burger King?"

Later that afternoon, she called Mel. "Have you talked to your mother?"

"Should I have?"

"I think so. I called her and told her the wedding was

in three weeks instead of six and she cut me off, saying that was 'unacceptable' and that she'd get back to me when she wasn't with a client. The ball is in your court now."

"Okay," he said in a dismal voice.

"How's the search for Miss Welbourne's children going?" she asked now that this was sorted out.

"Not well. Both newspapers I contacted said they wanted to put the pictures in the big Sunday edition that everybody has time to read, and the next issue was already too full to place it well."

"I'm sorry to hear that, but you can use some of your free time to call your mother now."

"What am I supposed to say?"

"That the date is set in stone. Four hundred guests is set in the same stone. I do all the flowers, she does the food, and we want the invitations to say no gifts are to be sent. And the charities they can contribute to."

"Is that really a good idea?" Mel said. "Somebody might give us something really nice. Like one of those really fancy outside grills."

"What we'll get is fourteen salad spinners, or eighteen sets of drinking glasses that don't match or four china soup tureens. You've seen my kitchen shelves. They're already crammed with what I use and need."

Mel gave up. "I have seen your kitchen shelves and if it were me, I'd give half of the things away. I see your point."

"We'll buy our own grill after the wedding though. I promise. And you get to choose it."

Jane assumed that Mel would corner his mother and Jane would deal with all of the flowers, and get on with life. Her agent had recommended that she set up a website and rent a post office box for fan mail. "You don't want fans, however nice they might be, to know where you live."

Jane had rented the post office box, but not yet tended to a website. She'd have to call Ted for suggestions of someone to do it for her. The Jeffry Pharmacy chain had a terrific website and she was pretty sure Ted hadn't done it himself.

Without fear, she could call him now that there was no chance of Thelma answering Ted's office phone. She'd call him later today.

All that remained of planning the wedding was picking up her hat, and getting the notice made up for the invitations that Jane and Mel didn't want gifts, just charitable donations. She'd recently priced business cards, but hadn't bought them yet, pending the website address. The owner of the place, however, had given her a reasonable price. She'd stop back today to buy the enclosures for the wedding announcements, send half to Addie and keep her half.

"Oops," she said aloud. One more important thing. Line up a judge to do the civil wedding now that the date was set.

Being a compulsive list maker, she got out her notebook she used for lists and rewrote the latest one with the judge in first place. Mel knew judges. But he was busy right now, so she'd call Uncle Jim instead.

"Uncle Jim, the date for the two weddings has changed," she said when she reached him. She could hear some kind of power tool grinding to a stop. He was taking this woodworking thing seriously now that he'd had a room added for doing it.

"Why's it changed?" he asked.

"Because Dad finished up early translating for the Danes. So they are coming earlier. Almost everything is set up for three weeks from now. But I need advice on one thing."

"Anything I can help with will be a pleasure," he said.

"I need to make an appointment with a judge to do the civil service before the big fat wedding happens. Addie, Mel's mother, is planning most of it."

"She's a terror."

"But a rich one. I've made rules. I chose all the flowers, I've chosen the hotel, and they can only supply rooms for three hundred guests."

"I don't think I even know three hundred people I'd want to invite to a wedding," Jim said with a laugh.

"Neither do I," Jane admitted. "But Addie wants to force all her richest clients into coming to 'her' wedding and eating and drinking well. Purely a business deal in her view."

"If she's paying for it, good for her. So when and where do Mel and I go to be fitted for tuxes?"

Jane consulted her notes and told him the answer. "Now, you tell me a good, pleasant judge we can prevail on to marry us."

Jim gave her three names, in order of preference, and told her their office phone numbers. He said again, "I can't wait to get to meet with your parents in person. It's been far too long since I've been able to just sit around and jaw with them."

"They feel the same way, Uncle Jim. And thanks for the names of judges. And by the way, would you take Todd along with you and Mel? Mike will have to go, too, the minute he gets home."

Two more revisions to the list, she thought.

Jane was pleased to cross a number of things off her list. The first judge she called was very impressed that Jim was her honorary uncle and would be glad to do the civil wedding. They set up a time.

The printing outfit she'd interviewed about business cards was glad to do the inserts for the wedding invitations. Jane instructed them that they should say, "Jane Jeffry and Mel VanDyne are combining households and don't need gifts. If guests wish to make a donation to Habitat for Humanity, the Red Cross, or the Salvation Army, Jane and Mel would be very grateful."

The printer suggested the printing style, the paper weight, and the color, and Jane accepted all of his advice. They would be ready by tomorrow.

Next on the list was picking up her hat. She still had a few quarters left; and the hat was ready and looked wonderful and wouldn't blow or fall off her head.

When she got back home, she called Ted about websites. He told her who had set up and updated the Jeffry

Pharmacy pages. "It's a bit expensive, but you won't have as much data to work with quite yet. Here's the name and number of the Webmaster."

She'd deal with this after the wedding, but was enormously smug at having tended to everything on her list. All she had to do was pick up the inserts for the wedding announcements the next day and FedEx half of them to Addie, then alert everybody involved as to where and when the civil wedding would take place.

A new list to make.

Chapter

TWENTY

Jane had finished everything on her list the day before, except calling the Webmaster Ted had suggested. That could wait until after the weddings. She started a new list. The fridge was nearly empty and after getting rid of some very overripe cheese and lumpy milk, and the last of the congealed inch of orange juice, she went hunting for other things that were way past their sell date. Some cream cheese that had never been opened and she feared it was too old to even examine closely.

Then she made a new list of meals and what she needed for each one. Chili sounded too hot for summer, and so was pot roast. Though she did both superbly in the winter. So she put down eggs, salad stuff, and good sourdough bread. Since the caper bottle had only four little mildewed globs, she also disposed of those and put them on the list along with a new bottle of salad dressing, mayo, and a variety of chips and soft drinks. Hamburger, hot dogs, bacon, and good summer tomatoes.

Then she rewrote the list by aisles in her closest grocery store. No point in wasting time going back to where she'd already been for something else.

Shelley was the only person who fully understood Jane's obsession with lists. Shelley sometimes made lists herself.

Jane came home with six bags. She had everything on the list, but she'd been drawn to some expensive little plastic bottles of pomegranate juice that she thought might be good for a special salad dressing she'd seen as a recipe in a magazine. She'd also bought some Ben and Jerry's Cherry Garcia ice cream. She hadn't purged the freezer, but she knew that Todd had eaten the last of the carton she thought she'd hidden to eat herself as a guilty pleasure from time to time.

There were some new interesting chips and crackers as well. Parmesan Cheez-Its, of all things. And great big Wheat Thins, and a bag of York Peppermint Patties, which weren't anywhere on the list, but were displayed next to the checkout line.

When she got home, she realized that the pantry also needed purging before she could put anything more in it. After hiding the ice cream behind a big bag of Texas Toast, she put away everything else that had to go in the fridge and started on the pantry.

There were soggy potato chips, three remaining Cheez-Its occupying a big box, Pringles that had also lost their crispness due to a missing lid, a box of Bisquick that felt solidified, many half-filled bags of various sizes and shapes of pastas, and three boxes of instant stuffing that had dates on the boxes that were three years old.

She was filling a trash bag when the phone rang.

Setting down the bag, she picked up the kitchen phone.

"Jane, it's Ted. Mother's gone."

"Oh, Ted. I'm so sorry," Jane said, trying hard to sound sincere.

"Jane, not even I am that sorry," Ted said.

"How did it happen? Another stroke?"

"Not exactly. There were protective plastic-covered bars around her bed to keep her from accidentally falling out of it. Apparently she'd been watching how the release button worked on the right side. She was only paralyzed on her left side. She apparently pressed the release button, and left her right arm between the bars, and catapulted out of the bed."

Jane smiled, and said, "Fighting life to the very last minute, wasn't she?"

Ted said, "It was what she did best." She could tell by his voice that he, too, was smiling.

"Was anybody in the room with her?" Jane asked.

"Yes, one of the younger nurses. The nurse tried to catch her, but Mother was half again the nurse's height and weight and broke several of the nurse's fingers on the fall.

Then she struck her head on the corner of the nightstand. They said she was dead before she even reached the floor."

"You're not thinking of bringing legal suit against the nursing home, are you?"

"Lord, *no*! Mother caused her own death, *and* injury to the nurse."

"She'll be buried next to your father, I assume."

"Yes, they bought four lots ages ago."

"Let me know when the funeral will be, please."

"Jane, you don't need to go. Dixie and the girls aren't even going. It's just going to be me and the church ladies. There will be a memorial service for our employees first."

"I need to be there to help you fend off the church ladies, Ted."

"I suppose that would help. I'll let you know the date as soon as I can."

The memorial service for the local employees was planned for Tuesday, and the burial for Wednesday. Ted asked Jane if she could write up this information and turn it in to several of the local newspapers.

It was the least she could do for Ted. Not Thelma.

She was especially careful not to let her personal opinion show. Or anything emotional. Just where and when Thelma Johnson Jeffry had been born to start the piece. Jane had asked for this information when Mike was born and she was filling in his baby book. Too bad Katie and Todd didn't have baby books. Between Mike's birth and Katie's she'd been too busy learning to be a cook, dishwasher, and diaper-changing mother.

Anyway, she had the information about Thelma, and said she was the widow of Elmer Jeffry, the founder of the Jeffry Pharmacy chain. Time and place of interment.

She faxed the notice to three newspapers, one of which was a county paper, with local school district schedules, sports events, local crimes of note, town picnics, and scholarships. The other newspapers were full of ads for jobs, notices of new local restrictions, lost pets, a list of local births, marriages, divorces, and funerals.

Jane called Mel and said, "It's Saturday and I've been to the grocery store. Please come for dinner. I'll have tons of summer food."

She didn't tell him about Thelma yet. It wasn't something to announce over the phone.

"How's my office coming along?"

"Swell. But it won't be ready for you until after the weddings, since the dates have been changed."

"I want to see it anyway. I'm starving. Can we eat at five?"

"Of course."

She prepared a big salad with pomegranate juice. The recipe called for one cup of juice, one cup of balsamic vinegar, a half teaspoon of olive oil, and one small egg yolk to emulsify it. Shake thoroughly, the recipe said. She took a taste when it was done and almost gasped at how good it was.

She also made deviled eggs, thin shaved ham, and brown mustard on egg rolls. She covered them with plastic wrap and would warm them up later. She invited

Shelley and Paul to come to dinner, but Paul was out of town on business. "Can my kids come along?"

"The more the merrier," Jane said. "I just bought more food than Todd and I can eat before it spoils. By the way, Thelma died in the nursing home today. I didn't want to tell you in front of the children. But I need to tell Todd as soon as he comes home from his summer class."

"Will he be upset?" Shelley asked.

"Probably not. I'll tell you why if you want to come over for a glass of raspberry-flavored iced tea."

Shelley agreed with Jane and Ted that Thelma had fought to the end. "She wasn't a nice woman. Do you suppose she ever was?"

"Well, she raised one good son. And another who wasn't."

On Wednesday, Jane insisted on driving Ted to the cemetery. "If I drive, I can rescue you from the church ladies. How did the company memorial service go yesterday?"

"Very well. My mother had written out a will about twelve years ago, at my insistence. She gave a gift of five hundred dollars to each manager of the pharmacies. Of course there were only four of them at that time, and now there are twelve. So everybody was happy."

"Would you be comfortable telling me about the rest of the bequests?" Jane asked.

"Of course. Since it's not a trust, it's not private. She gave the church a thousand dollars, and her third share of the profits to me. Since she never expected us to adopt children, there was no per stirpes mentioned. So our girls will inherit my share."

"Ted, I'm so relieved to hear that. Especially since she had wills in mind and tried to forge an amendment to Steve's. And it's much, much better that your lovely little girls will have a good financial future someday."

When they drove into the driveway to the cemetery, it was almost blocked with cars. The members of the church Thelma belonged to had turned out in droves. That would have pleased Thelma. As Jane pulled into the remaining parking area, she realized they'd been followed through the gates by the black cars of the funeral establishment.

She'd always thought the procession of these cars was touching and dignified. She and Ted walked over to the grave site that Ted's father Elmer had bought decades ago for the whole family. There were rows of chairs set up around a deep grave that was covered with a white cloth.

She noticed that the other people were almost entirely elderly women. Many of them as hard-faced and tough as Thelma. There was a scattered group of old men, mostly with walkers or in wheelchairs. There were also a few very short, tiny old women with dowager humps. They hadn't had access to drugs that kept their spines from collapsing.

The service was relatively short. Many cloth handkerchiefs were raised to the ladies' faces. There were a huge number of floral tributes set around the sides of the grave. When the coffin was lowered, Jane glanced at Ted. His face showed no emotion whatsoever. He clearly wasn't grief stricken, but not showing what was probably a sense of relief either.

After the service, some of the stronger ladies took along a few of the floral tributes saying they'd look so good at the church. Most of them approached Ted, expressing their sympathy, which he accepted with grace. The last two to speak to him were two of the tougher women, one of whom said, "We're going back to church for a meal made for the mourners. You will be attending, won't you, Mr. Jeffry?"

"I'm afraid I can't. I'm meeting with our attorney this afternoon to sort out the donations my mother specified. There is one for the church, I'm glad to say."

"How nice of your mother. When will we know how much?"

"Soon," Ted said.

Another of the tiny ladies then came and took Ted's hand in both of hers, smiling. Jane thought she must have probably been the prettiest girl in school. And in spite of her wrinkles and abundant white hair, she still looked very good.

She said, "I was hoping to see your wife and your darling babies here."

"She couldn't find a babysitter for the girls," Ted said.

"Oh, dear. We should have thought of providing one for you." She turned to Jane and said, "I remember you, Ms. Jeffry. I've missed seeing you and your children at church."

"Two of them go to school and have summer jobs in other states," Jane said, shaking her hand. "I remember you, too, Mrs. Jefferson. You were their Sunday school teacher and they adored you. So did I."

"How sweet of you. I hope we'll meet again. And my deepest sympathies to you, Mr. Jeffry. Your mother must have been a handful to work with."

He smiled. "She certainly was."

"I must go," Mrs. Jefferson said. "I'm supposed to supply the lemonade and it's probably getting hot in my car. Best wishes to both of you."

The moment she turned away, he took Jane by the elbow, thanked the pastor, and swiftly headed toward Jane's car.

"Well done, Ted. You didn't need my help after all."

"I knew you would if it was necessary though. That's what counts."

"Will you and Dixie and the girls come to dinner with us tonight? I have lots of food."

"That would be wonderful. I'll have to check with Dixie, but I'm sure she'll agree."

"Mrs. Jefferson is one of the good ones from the church."

"One of the few," Ted said with a smile as he got into Jane's car.

Chapter

TWENTY-ONE

Dixie looked five years younger than the last time Jane had seen her, and she was smiling and making the little girls laugh when she made funny faces. Ted looked happier and more relaxed than ever now that Thelma's funeral was over. It was a lovely evening and everyone ate heartily. After dinner she showed them around Mel's new office, which was finally looking like it might turn out to be done in a couple of weeks. Then he could choose the carpet and paint colors, and move his office furniture in.

Ted said, "This makes me think it's time to renovate my own office at work. It hasn't changed for years and everything looks old and dingy."

"Oh, Ted," Dixie said, "that's a wonderful idea. Can I help you pick out new furniture and paint colors?"

"You'll have to. I have no idea how to do this," he said. "Anything that isn't dark brown. And I have to clean out my mother's house to sell it. Do either of you want anything from it? A favorite lamp or some of her jewelry?"

Dixie looked at him and said, "I wouldn't want anything she'd ever touched."

Jane chimed in. "There's nothing I want either."

"So what do I do with her jewelry? She has a lot of it, and some is valuable. Her wedding ring has a huge diamond—"

Jane stepped up to the bat before Dixie could speak. "Take them to an appraiser, and find out what they're worth. Then sell them on eBay or a local jeweler."

"What a good idea, Jane," Dixie piped up. "Now let's don't talk about this anymore, Ted. Make your own decisions, and don't even tell me about them." She was smiling as she said this.

Dixie turned to where the girls were sitting in their high chairs, and said, "I'm right, aren't I?" She nodded her head and both of the girls laughed and tried to imitate the gesture. Mary, who was a year and a half old, dribbled orange juice all over her pink dress. Sarah, at four years, got it right.

Ted was grinning.

Jane called Mel when Ted, Dixie, and the girls had left. She told him about the nice dinner and then asked, "How's your case going?"

"Which one?"

"The Welbournes, of course."

"Not much yet. Both reporters have told me that they've had a lot of calls, but they're all either frauds, or someone who claims to have met them two years ago in Perth, or Sydney, or Orlando. But somebody will turn up knowing how to spell Miss Welbourne's whole name. Then we move in."

Jane went to bed that night thinking about Ted and Dixie. Thelma's death was, sadly, the best thing that ever happened to them. They had both been so relaxed and pleasant at dinner. The relief of not having Thelma around, making their lives miserable, must have been enormous. And would only get better over time.

Then she started thinking about herself. This was Wednesday. At the end of next week, she'd be married. Her parents were arriving next Thursday. Next Wednesday her parents would be packing for the long flight from Denmark to New York then the short one to Chicago. Her dad would send his documents from the meetings in Denmark to Washington.

Thursday Mike would be driving home from Indiana, and Katie would be flying in from Kansas. The civil wedding would be on Friday, and Addie's wedding would be Saturday at five in the afternoon. Suddenly, she realized how close it all was—finally. It was a shame Mel's office wouldn't be ready in time. But that wasn't so important. He'd already hired people to take away his office furniture three weeks after the weddings.

Everything was finally coming together.

Unless Addie ruined it.

Meanwhile, Jane could happily work on the details of her new book. The planning was just as invigorating as the actual writing was. She loved the surprises that her mind served up from time to time during that process.

The week seemed to crawl along though. Every day seemed longer. And hotter. The workers were now putting in windows. The necessary door to the outside in case of fire in the house was completed. But the flooring hadn't arrived, though it had been promised earlier. The outside hadn't been stuccoed yet. They'd considered brick, but it was far more expensive.

Jane hadn't ever heard back from Addie and didn't know if she was coming to the real wedding. But it was a matter of pride not to call her back. Mel was unable to reach her either. But he wasn't worried. He claimed she was a busy woman. She'd show up in time, he assured Jane.

Jane did call the hotel billing department, asking if Addie VanDyne had paid for the hotel booking. She was told that all they'd received was a hefty down payment.

This worried Jane, and even slightly alarmed Mel when she told him. "I'll pay for it if she doesn't," Jane said.

"No. You won't. I'll hunt her down if I have to drive down there and hammer on her door."

She didn't ask him until two days later if his mother

had paid. "She claimed she did," Mel said. "You might ask if the hotel has gotten it."

"You can do that," Jane said. She knew she was being a bit snippy, and apologized. "Never mind. I don't have a 'real' job like you do. I'll call."

"Jane, this isn't your responsibility. I will find out. I'm sorry I tried to shove this off on you. You *do* have a real job. And it's a more interesting one than mine."

It was turning into a battle of apologies, and she didn't know how to stop it.

Mel called back an hour later. "Janey, the hotel has already cashed the check. If it doesn't bounce, we're home free." The "Janey" part of this statement eased her mind. At least he wasn't mad at her. And she had probably deserved criticism for her nervous behavior.

"Could I persuade you to take me to a nice dinner? On my nickel? I'm desperate to eat something I didn't cook for myself. Can't your Officer Needham monitor any calls you get about the Welbournes? You can take along your cell phone and abandon me if something important comes in."

"That sounds good. I've been living on sandwiches and chips in the canteen."

This time they decided not to go to their favorite expensive restaurant and settled for a chain restaurant with a salad bar. Mel made himself an enormous salad and two rolls. Jane had a shrimp and pasta dish. They were sitting in a corner booth and since they'd gone early, nobody was close to them.

She was determined not to mention his mother, but Mel himself started talking about her after he'd eaten.

"She was tough on me. Wanted me to be a stockbroker so I'd get rich. Every time she got pregnant, I'd wish for another brother to take some of the stress off me. But all I got were sisters. She liked them okay, but made them always dress alike in pink dresses or shorts and shirts. They now wear black, mostly. Just to get back at her, I suspect."

"Pink? How horrible. And dressing all the same, like replicas of each other."

"She was livid when I graduated from college and wanted to go into law enforcement. She thought it was a dirty, nasty job, dealing only with scummy criminals. She wouldn't pay for it. So I put myself through college waiting tables, mowing lawns, pet sitting, and slinging hash at a breakfast place."

"You've never told me about this," Jane said. "Why not?"

"I never thought I'd need to. To this day, she's disappointed in me, and tells her clients and friends that I am a very successful stockbroker."

"Is this why she also dislikes me?"

"No. She thinks of you as a dumb housewife, spending your time at grocery stores and dress shops."

"Have you ever told her the truth? That I've raised three brilliant kids, and have a job and a very good income?"

"I haven't. It's really not any of her business. She pretends that what's wrong with marrying you is that you're two years older than I am. As if that matters to either of us."

176

Jane smiled. "At least she's not as outright nasty as my other mother-in-law was."

"And she doesn't live anywhere close to you," Mel said.

"Yes, you're right. That's one benefit."

Mel said, "Want a dessert?"

"Yes. Something with gooey hot fudge if it's on the menu."

While they were waiting for dessert, Mel made a prediction. "I suspect this trip for our wedding is probably the last time she'll ever be in Chicago to visit us. And I'll bet you ten dollars she refuses to come to your house to see the office you're building for me."

"That's a bet I wouldn't make. I'm sure you're right. And it's a relief that you don't seem to mind."

"I don't mind at all. When she grows too old to run around selling real estate, she's going to be a very lonely person. She's hasn't earned much loyalty from her children. That's another thing I love about you. Your kids would go to the wall to please you."

Jane teared up at this compliment.

Chapter

❀

TWENTY-TWO

Mike was the first to arrive. He'd asked his professor for a couple of extra days to spend time with his mother.

He was a bit shocked to discover that Todd had taken over his bedroom. So he just dumped his own stuff in what had been Todd's room.

"How's it going, Mom?" he asked as he galloped back down the stairs.

"Fairly well," she said mildly. "But you need to go and be fitted for a tux today."

"Okay, I'll do it now if you tell me what are all those papers stuck to your dining room window?" Mike said.

"They're permits. Come out in the backyard and see what's going on."

"Jeez," he exclaimed. "What's that big room for?"

"Mel's home office. He had a room in his apartment for working at home, so I'm giving him one here."

Mike moved closer to look through an unfinished section. "Even a bathroom. Mom, have you spent our whole inheritance on this?"

She laughed. "Just part of it. Uncle Jim has retired and had the same architect and contractor add a woodworking room for him. So I latched onto the same men. Since the weddings have been moved up by three weeks, it won't be finished in time."

"Weddings, plural?"

"Yes. On Friday the family goes to a judge's chamber for a civil wedding, then Saturday is Addie's blowout wedding."

"Why did you let her take charge?"

"To save part of your inheritance. She's paying for the hotel rental, and the food, and the band for dancing later."

"Still, that's not right."

"It's okay by me. Free food. Free band for a dance afterward, and also a free dinner for the rehearsal dinner, which *is* her responsibility."

Mike just shrugged. "I guess that does make sense. When do Grumps and Nana get here?"

"Thursday. Katie's staying with them at the hotel. I've sent a car service to take her at four. Your grandparents arrive tomorrow at ten in the morning. Would you want to come along with me to the airport to pick them up?"

"It will have to be in your car. I won't force them to ride in the back of my truck. So, when is Mel's awful mother arriving?"

"We have no idea. And I'm not going to ask."

"You don't know when she's coming? You don't know if she's paid for hijacking your wedding?"

"Second and fake wedding. I've checked with the hotel and she has made a full payment. So I assume she'll probably come, just to get something to eat that she's paid for."

"What about the rest of it? Flowers and stuff like that."

"I'm paying for all the flowers. And I've alerted the hotel planner that if Addie tries to stuff the front with bridesmaids and groomsmen, they have to sit with everyone else."

"Mom, when did you get so tough?"

"When you quit mowing my lawn and Katie quit cooking for us." Jane laughed. "And I no longer have to put up with Grandma Thelma. That was a huge relief."

"Was she giving you trouble?"

"Lots of it. She tried to forge an addendum to your father's will saying if I remarried, I'd cease to get my third of the pharmacy profits."

Mike opened his mouth and nothing came out for a minute or two. "You squashed that, I hope."

"I told her that if she tried to get away with it, I'd take her to court for fraud and forgery. She'd become so much more bitter and combative over the last few years."

"I'm glad I wasn't around to have to endure her. She's always been nasty to me."

"You, too?"

"Because I once told her I wanted to be a plant patent attorney. She only heard the 'plant' word and jumped all over me about having nothing but a gardening job."

"Why didn't you tell me this before?"

"Because I knew you'd go ballistic."

Jane grinned. "I guess I would have. Let's don't even talk about her anymore. It's too upsetting. You and Todd decide where you want to go for dinner. I don't want to labor over a hot stove in this heat."

After Mike came home with a tux that fit perfectly without any changes, Todd and Mike decided dinner should be at an Italian restaurant. Later, when the three of them got out of the car, Jane realized that the building was huge. "Have you made reservations?"

"Oh, Mom. We're not stupid. It's a huge buffet and you can choose from about fifty different things, and even go back for seconds."

"How did you know about this, Todd?"

"Elliot invited me along with his family two or three weeks ago. Don't you remember that?"

"Sure. But you never said where you'd gone. Let's go in. I'm starving."

By the time they'd eaten, Jane was stuffed to the gills. She'd started with bruschetta and a big salad with grilled chicken. Then she went back for spaghetti and meatballs, and finished with tiramisu.

"Do they have gurney service to the curb?" she asked her boys.

"Probably not," Mike said, "but if you want we could roll you to the car."

When they returned home, Jane was feeling the results of eating so much. She decided to go to bed early. Tomorrow would probably be a long day.

Unfortunately, she couldn't get to sleep. Her stomach was hurting. So she got back up and took a few Tums. That seemed to help. And by eleven she was sound asleep. But her last thought before sleeping was that she had to be up early to go to the airport with Mike to pick up her parents. She set her alarm for seven in the morning.

She woke moments before the alarm went off, feeling better, but not quite up to normal. She took a quick shower and dressed, then went downstairs to make a very bland, unbuttered piece of toast, and another two Tums. Soon she felt like her usual self. Perky and feeling good about what a nice day it would be, seeing her parents after a long time. Almost two years since they'd been to Chicago.

Mike drove his mother's Jeep, since he knew his mother hated parking at the airport. He'd just drop her off. "You have your cell phone, right?"

"I do."

"And is it charged?"

Jane gave him a slitty-eyed sideways glance. "It is."

"Call me when you have their luggage out the door, and I'll cruise around until I find you."

Jane opened the passenger door in a distinctly huffy manner and was muttering as she walked into the airport. "Is your cell phone charged?" Had Mike, a full-fledged adult in law school, decided that his mother was becoming a bit dotty?

She had no ticket and wasn't allowed to meet her parents at the plane. So she went down to the baggage area and took a paperback mystery novel out of her purse. Luckily, the plane was on time, and she kept looking up at intervals watching people coming down the escalators. Soon she spotted them and raced to the right baggage carousel. Stuff was already coming off as she hugged and kissed her mother.

She's gone gray, Jane thought, *and it suits her with that short curly hair.* Her dad waited until his wife and daughter finished hugging and gave Jane a big bear hug. "You're looking good," he said. "Are you a nervous bride?"

"Not nervous, but a bit harassed. You got my e-mails about Thelma trying to trick me and then going to a nursing home and dying?"

"That must be a huge relief to you," her mother said.

"It was. But I had to go to the funeral with Ted. Dixie wouldn't go and I thought he needed a woman along to defend him from the church ladies."

"Oh, here comes our luggage, Michael. Can you find a trolley to get it outside?"

In a minute or two, Jane's dad was back. And Jane realized that they'd brought an enormous number of bags stuffed to brimming and even two medium-size trunks.

She didn't dare ask until they were in the car. She called Mike and said, "We're taking the luggage outside right now," and in a whisper, added, "There's a whole lot of it."

Mike pulled up, opening the back door of the Jeep, and hugged each grandparent. Then he started loading up the back section of the Jeep. He was half afraid it wouldn't all go in but managed to wrestle it in after moving a few things around twice to make them fit.

"Michael, you ride in front with Mike, and I'll ride back here with Jane," Cecily said.

As they pulled out onto the highway, Mike asked, "Why are you guys so loaded down with luggage and trunks?" Michael turned his head and winked at Cecily.

"Should we tell them now?"

"Why not?" Jane's mother said. "It wasn't meant to be a secret. Michael and I are officially retired. Now we can finally settle down somewhere, and we thought Chicago would be perfect."

"I'm thrilled to hear this," Jane said. "House or condo?"

"Condo," Cecily said. "Neither of us has ever mowed grass and we don't want to learn how to."

Michael said, "We're starved. All we ate today was a bag of potato chips on the plane from New York."

"Let's stop off on the way home," his grandson said.

"A good Mexican restaurant, please," Cecily said. "The Danes aren't hot on Mexican food and I'm longing for some."

Jane was sorry she hadn't brought her bottle of Tums along. And felt a tad gaggy at the thought of Mexican food after all she'd eaten the night before. Maybe she could make do with chips and a mild queso.

Chapter

❀

TWENTY-THREE

Jane, Mike, Cecily, and Michael were waiting in the lobby of the hotel for Katie to arrive.

Jane had explained to her parents that she'd booked them into a two-bedroom suite because Katie wanted to stay with them.

When Katie arrived with a rather large suitcase, she set it down and rushed across the lobby. "Mom, they picked me up in a white stretch limo as if I were a celebrity."

She set down the suitcase with a thud and embraced her grandparents and then her mother. Mike edged away from a hug.

Jane said, "Someday you will be a celebrity chef."

"Right now I'm starving," Katie said.

Jane had a bellhop take Katie's monster suitcase up to the suite and they all went into the deli restaurant in the hotel.

When they'd picked out sandwiches and chips, Katie asked, "So what's the plan?"

"The rehearsal dinner here tonight. A civil wedding tomorrow morning. Just family. Then Addie's wedding at five the next day."

"What do you mean by 'Addie's wedding'?" Katie asked. Jane explained.

"That's stupid. She's not the bride's mother," Katie complained. "She's Mel's mother."

"As I've already pointed out to Mike, it saves me the money," Jane said with a laugh.

"Wait until you guys see what Mom's doing to her house, speaking of spending money."

Cecily asked, "What are you doing, Jane?"

"Adding an office for Mel in back of the dining room," Jane said.

"I think that's nice," her father said.

"Thank you, Dad. Mike doesn't like it."

"Yes, I do," Mike objected. "I just think you're spending too much money."

"Mike, it's *my* money, and Mel is moving from an apartment where one bedroom was his office. He needs one at our house when he moves in."

"We need to all take a rest and then dress for the rehearsal dinner," Jane said. "It's in this hotel somewhere. I'll go ask where and when."

Jane was back in moments with printed instructions for finding the right place and time. She gave one copy to her mother and kept the other one.

They were all on time for the rehearsal dinner in the hotel. Addie had brought along her two daughters, Alice and Emily, and their husbands, who were also introduced. Mel was introduced last.

Jane then took her turn, "My parents, Michael and Cecily Grant. My son Mike, my daughter, Katie, and my son Todd. And this wonderful gentleman is my honorary uncle, Jim Harding."

The whole time Jane was speaking, and pointing out the family members, Addie had her eyes on Cecily with an expression that was a mix of envy and hostility.

My mother is prettier, nicer, and more sophisticated than you are, and you know it, Addie, Jane was thinking.

Addie finally tore her eyes away from Cecily and said, "I have labels on the table by the door. Please put your names on them so anybody who didn't catch all of them will know you."

Drinks were served with trays of appetizers, while the hot food was being brought in from the kitchen. The food was ordinary and rather sparse but tasty, despite coming from the hotel kitchen. There wasn't a vegetarian choice of meals. Addie apparently didn't care much about food—at least for this meal intended for family.

There was a choice of two desserts, both of which contained walnuts, which Jane herself hated, so she passed. There wasn't even a groom's cake.

Altogether it was boring food, and the only people who seemed to be enjoying themselves were Jane's own kids. Even Addie merely picked at her plate. Jane put her left arm on her lap and looked at her watch. An hour and a half wasted. Mel, sitting next to her, patted her right hand and whispered, "It's almost over. Fifteen minutes and we'll be out of here."

He proved to be right. He stood up and announced that he and Jane had enjoyed themselves and graciously thanked his mother for a nice dinner. He stood up and took Jane's hand to depart. Everyone else bolted out right behind them, except for Addie, who was actually tipping the employees.

Almost all the same people attended the civil ceremony the next morning, even though they weren't part of the wedding party. Jane had only invited Mel's mother, her parents and her kids, Uncle Jim, and Shelley. Addie had forced her daughters and their husbands to attend as well, which put the participants cheek to jowl in the small room. It only took fifteen minutes to say the vows, and sign the wedding certificate.

"Sorry, Janey," Mel said when his own family had departed. "I told her it was only for the people in the wedding and she dragged along another four people who aren't part of it."

"Don't worry. It's over. And we're married. Do I have to give the wedding ring back so you give it to me again tomorrow?"

"Probably. I'll give mine back to you as well."

On Saturday morning Jane persuaded Shelley to come with her to the hotel, just to check out anything that might go wrong.

"What could go wrong?" Shelley asked.

"With Addie involved, a lot of things could go bad."

Shelley shrugged. "Okay. You might have a point."

They found Miss Tarlington, who was looking at Jane rather oddly. "We've already set the tables for dinner. Would you like to come look? There are twenty tables for ten. Mrs. Nowack was right. Only a hundred and forty-nine of Mrs. VanDyne's guests are attending."

They followed her. Shelley whispered to Jane, "I think that she's worried."

Jane nodded.

When the door to the dining area opened, both she and Shelley gasped.

"What on earth are those flowers on the tables?"

"They aren't what you ordered?" Miss Tarlington asked.

The vases were tall and bright blue, with calla lilies and ferns.

"No, they aren't. Where did these come from?" Jane asked.

Miss Tarlington told Jane the name of the florist.

"That's not my florist. Mine is coming at two with low bowls of gardenias."

"Thank goodness, Ms. Jeffry, I knew you had better sense and taste than this. Nobody could see over them to the people across the table."

Shelley spoke up in a faint voice. "So what do we do with them? Can the wrong florist come back and take them away?"

"I doubt it," Miss Tarlington said.

"Please check," Jane said. "And if this florist won't pick them up, can you find someone on the staff to load them up and take them to the nursing home where my mother-in-law was? I don't have my address book with me, but I'll call it in as soon as I get home."

"There will be a charge for that."

"Naturally there will be. And Mrs. VanDyne can pay it."

"I suppose you'd like to also see the bridal bouquet?"

"Oh no! Not that as well?"

Miss Tarlington took Jane and Shelley back to a kitchen where there was a glass house for flowers waiting to be put out. "There it is," she said, pointing to a massive bouquet of huge pink roses.

Jane put her hands over her eyes for a moment then looking again, she said, "Get rid of it. It must weigh ten pounds and would clash horribly with my suit."

"I can find somewhere in the lobby to put this monster," Miss Tarlington said. "It will have to go in a really big vase."

"Could you wait until the wedding is over so she doesn't recognize it as she comes in?"

"Good idea, Ms. Jeffry."

When they were back in Shelley's van, Shelley said, "What a hell of a nerve Addie has. She's known from the start you were doing your flowers, and probably thought that she could get away with doing them herself without your knowing in time."

"I'm so glad I had a premonition that something might go wrong," Jane said. "You're right. If we hadn't seen them in time, it would have been a disaster."

"Are you going to rat on her to Mel?"

"No. He'd just be even madder at her. He probably forgot about the flowers after he told her the rules. But I'd sent her a copy that she must have thrown away in a fit of pique."

As soon as she got home, Jane called Miss Tarlington with the address of the nursing home.

She went back out again to have her hair done, and even asked them if they did makeup as well. It was a day spa, so she got lucky. And she didn't look like a tart or an owl. She looked like herself, but better.

Jane and Shelley were back at the hotel earlier than they needed to be just to check once again that the right florist had brought the proper flower arrangements for the tables. As they opened the door to the room they could smell the lovely scent of the gardenias.

"You and your florist made an excellent choice," Shelley said.

"He did a wonderful job. We need to go to room 5200 for the pictures to be taken ahead of time, remember?"

"I do. But we don't have to be there until three o'clock."

"Let's go get glasses of iced tea and take them with us," Jane suggested.

"I've already checked into a room. You need to bring your suitcase in and check in as well. I've ordered soft drinks and iced tea and coffee to be sent to suite 5200 where the pictures will be taken," Shelley said.

"Oh, Shelley, how good of you."

When they entered suite 5200, Mel was already there, and so was his mother.

"Janey, you look fabulous," he said before he gave her a quick kiss. "And you smell wonderful."

Addie was sitting in a chair sipping a glass of iced tea and said nothing.

A moment or two later, Jane's parents arrived, with all three of Jane's children. Mike and Todd looked so good in their tuxes that Jane got misty. Katie was wearing a long yellow dress and matching sandals. Jane had never seen this outfit before. "You look wonderful. Where did you find such a pretty dress and shoes?"

"At Nordstrom—on sale," Katie answered smugly.

The pastor who was doing the service followed Katie in. "What handsome people you are. The photographer is coming along behind me."

A man loaded down with a big bag arrived a minute later. "Is everybody here? I'm not late, am I?"

Jane soothed him. "We're all early."

He set up his camera on a tripod and started with Jane and Mel alone. Then with Jane and her family, then Mel and his family. He was taking three pictures of each group just so they'd have a choice in case someone had their eyes closed.

After this, he grouped them all in front of a wall of

draped windows and pushed them around until he was satisfied. Then he took three more pictures.

Miss Tarlington showed up and said, "It's time to go. I need to show the wedding party where to stay until the guests are all in place."

They followed her in a private elevator that took them directly to the floor where the wedding would be held. There were soft chairs, two coffee tables with bowls of mints and glasses of water.

"I'll be back for you shortly," Miss Tarlington said.

Jane suddenly realized someone was missing. "Shelley, where is Paul?"

"He had an emergency in Miami. There was a fire in the kitchen and he had to take the insurance policy and some other paperwork down there last night."

"Oh, that's too bad. I really hoped he'd be here."

Shelley said, "So did I."

They could hear people in the hallway outside the room chatting as they were passing through to the wedding room. Jane had seen it before. It was set up with pews like a church but without any sense of a particular religion. They waited until they couldn't hear anyone else in the hallway. Miss Tarlington came to fetch them, and line them up properly. She took Mel and Uncle Jim down a side hall, opened a door, and said, "You stand on the left side and face forward."

She went back and took Todd and Mike, and Michael and Cecily next.

Jane and Shelley were standing in the back behind a door.

They peered around and saw Mike take his grandmother's arm and start down the aisle with Michael following. They were seated in the first pew on the right. Then Todd took Addie's arm with her daughters and their husbands following them to the front pew on the left.

Then Shelley walked down by herself.

There was a brief wait while Mike took his mother's arm and escorted her to the front next to Shelley. Jane was surprised that everyone stood and looked back at them with big smiles.

The ceremony itself was relatively short. Rings were exchanged for the second time. Mel took Jane in his arms and gave her a serious but dignified kiss. A sound system burst into "Here Comes the Bride" and the two of them walked back slowly, stopping to shake hands with a number of people close to the center aisle. Mel was well represented with what looked like half the police force, some in uniform, most in plain suits.

Jane and Mel stood beside the door, while Todd and Mike escorted the Grants, Katie, and Addie's family back down the aisle. Uncle Jim brought Shelley down the aisle. Then everybody else was left to file out neatly from front to back and be pointed to the dining room by Miss Tarlington. Some of Mel's friends hung back to congratulate Mel and Jane. A few of Addie's rich clients stopped to compliment her as well. She smiled and thanked them for coming, then joined the rest of the crowd, ignoring the whole of Jane's family. Jane could hear Mel grinding his teeth and muttering.

The rest of the family went to the dining room, leaving Jane and Mel alone for a minute or two. "I'm sorry, Mel. But you know the way she acts. It's normal for her."

"You're right. It's sad though."

They made their way, arm in arm, to the dining room, and again everyone stood up and applauded. When they sat down, Miss Tarlington spoke into a microphone. "Someone at each table will find a penny concealed in their napkin. Mr. and Mrs. VanDyne have told me that those who get one are entitled to take the flowers on the table home."

There was a great rush to open napkins.

The wedding party was already seated, and Addie got up and leaned over Jane's shoulder, "What happened to my flowers?"

"They've gone to a nursing home. I'd told you repeatedly that I was choosing my flowers." Then she turned to Mel and asked, "Did you get the penny?"

Addie had apparently wanted to please her clients so much that she'd provided three courses: salad, choice of salmon or filet mignon, scalloped potatoes, asparagus, and an array of desserts on a buffet at the back of the room for later.

Addie had provided a huge wedding cake and Mel and Jane did the obligatory cutting of the first slice and feeding each other a bite. When the waiters started clearing tables, Mel and Jane circulated. Jane had invited very few people. Ted's wife and children, and the nice lady, Mrs. Jefferson, from Thelma's funeral, and a very few neighbors and women she'd known from the room mother's group.

Mel made a point of introducing her to his assistant, Officer Needham, who was wearing a bright red suit and a big matching hat. Jane said Mel had told her what a great researcher he thought she was and Jane hauled her along to meet her parents and children.

Eventually the room was cleared and guests were herded into the room where the dance was to be held. Some of the guests starting slipping away. And as Mel took her arm for the first dance, Officer Needham, ear to her cell phone, whispered something to him.

His response was a huge grin. "I'm going to dance with my wife while you gather up the team."

"What's this about?" Jane asked as they started to dance.

"The reporter from the *New York Times* has found Miss Welbourne's children. Or we think they are."

"Where are they?"

"Right here in Chicago. They're living in a rental in Evanston. They never left the area. That trip to San Francisco was a sham. Janey, I'm so sorry but—"

"It's your job, Mel. I understand. Now go! I'll dance with Uncle Jim, my dad, and Ted instead." When she'd finished dancing with them, she went to find Mrs. Jefferson, the nice church lady she'd met at Thelma's funeral. "I guess you learned to waltz when you were a girl. Would you do this next dance with me?"

Mrs. Jefferson smiled. "I learned dancing at a girls' school. I still remember."

When Jane and Mrs. Jefferson took the floor, other couples backed away, smiling. The photographer took several pictures, and other guests who'd brought cameras along joined in. As soon as the waltz was over, Jane bowed to Mrs. Jefferson and stood beside her, holding hands as others took more pictures. Both ladies did a curtsy. Jane then asked Mrs. Jefferson if she needed a ride home. "Ted Jeffry doesn't drink. He'd be glad to take you."

"No, thank you, Mrs. Jeff—I mean Mrs. VanDyne. My grandson is arriving to fetch me in a few minutes."

Jane stayed in what was supposed to be the honeymoon suite. She didn't mind that the groom wasn't there. He was doing his job. If she'd ever had the chance to be sent on a book tour, she wouldn't dream of making him take time off to go with her.

Besides, she'd packed a bag with the clothes she'd come here in and others she intended to wear the next day. She had her makeup and vitamins along. Her mother called Jane at nine the next morning. "Jane, dear, that waltz with the pretty old lady was the highlight of the wedding. I'm so proud of you for singling her out."

"She was the only nice woman at Thelma's funeral and I wanted to give her a tribute."

"I take it as a tribute to your father and me as well for raising such a nice thoughtful woman."

"You and Dad did a good job of teaching me good manners."

"Have you heard from Mel?" Cecily asked, changing the subject.

"Not a word. Where are we having breakfast?"

"We might as well just eat at the hotel. I stepped outside a few minutes ago and it's really too hot to walk somewhere else."

"I'll meet you as soon as I can catch an elevator."

Her mother, father, and Katie were waiting for her as she emerged.

"Did you invite Todd and Mike?" Jane asked.

"They're already here, holding a table for us."

As they entered the dining room, Todd hopped up and pulled his mother aside. "Mike had too much champagne and let me drive his truck home. It was cool. When are you going to buy me a truck? You bought his. I remember that."

"Katie doesn't have a car yet. You have to wait your turn," Jane said, taking his arm and leading him to the table.

As Jane sat down, Katie asked, "Why did Mel disappear from the wedding after the first dance?"

"Because he'd been waiting for some people to be found and somebody found them."

"Who are they?" Katie asked.

"You'll have to ask him about it later."

"How much later?"

Jane just shrugged and said, "Nobody knows. And he might not want to talk about it yet."

"But you know, Mom?"

"Just a little of it. I'm starving," she said, picking up the breakfast menu.

When they'd ordered and were waiting for the food to arrive, Jane asked her father, "Have you told your plans to Katie yet?"

"Yes, if you mean that we intend to live in Chicago soon. I have a few last reports to make before I can be let go to be retired."

"Are you sure you don't want to buy a house?" Jane said.

Her mother laughed at this. "My darling daughter, we've never owned a house. We don't know how to mow lawns, or cook for ourselves, or remember when to pay the water bill."

"Most certainly," her father added. "We need something with a concierge, and maybe a cook who can also teach us how to cook."

Cecily raised an elegant eyebrow and said, "You're going to learn this?"

Michael laughed. "I thought maybe you might take the lessons."

Cecily simply smiled.

When breakfast was done, Jane asked, "Would you like to take us all along to look at some condos?"

"That would be fine," Michael said. "But we'd have to hire a car service to haul all of us."

Katie had been looking back and forth from her grandmother to her grandfather. "Do either of you know how to drive or have a driver's license?"

"We both know how to drive, and have licenses from a half dozen different countries, including America. But we will need to buy a car."

"Can I go with you to pick one out?" Mike asked eagerly.

His grandfather had no time to answer because two waiters were putting down their plates.

When they were finished eating and had paid the bill, Jane's father said instead of looking for condos they wanted to see the office she was building for Mel. Mike and Todd took Mike's truck, and Jane took her parents and Katie home in her Jeep.

The work was admired. "When will it be done?" her father asked.

"It was supposed to be done when we got married, but since we moved the date forward, Mel will have to wait to move his things."

As she spoke, the phone rang and she rushed back inside to catch the call.

"Janey," Mel said. "Where and when are all of you having dinner? And may I join you?"

"I'd love that. They're all here looking at your office. Nobody's working on it because it's Sunday. Is your mother still here?"

"Nope. She escaped first thing this morning."

Jane was tempted to show her relief, but managed to

sound sorry. "She won't get to see your office today."

"Dinner, Jane? I've only had an Egg McMuffin for breakfast. And it was early."

When she called back to tell him where they'd decided to go, he said, "Let me pick you up so I can talk to you privately."

"You've found them, haven't you?"

"We have. The brother is in big trouble. We're hoping his sister will try to save herself by spilling the beans."

Epilogue

First," Mel explained, "the brother and sister were surprised that two people, one in a tux and the other in a red dress and hat, were beating on their door at one in the morning with three uniformed, armed men standing behind them."

That made Jane laugh.

"They were completely befuddled and so dim that they invited us all inside. I asked them if the house was a rental and if so, who owned it. The brother, if he really is Miss Welbourne's son, rummaged in his billfold for the owner's business card and gave it to me. I handed it over to Officer Needham and she went outside to call and wake the owner up. She asked him when the Welbournes had rented the house."

"And when was it?" Jane asked.

"A week before Miss Welbourne was murdered."

"Time to find out where she lived and where she worked?" Jane asked.

"Maybe. Welbourne said he'd been to the barbershop that morning and while waiting looked through an old copy of the *New York Times*, and saw the picture of himself and his sister.

"Then I asked them if they'd dress and come down to the police station and again, they stupidly, or cannily, agreed. I left two of the other officers to stay at the house until the judge, who wasn't happy to be woken up in the middle of the night, signed a warrant to search the house."

"What did they find?"

"The blackjack. In a small black Dopp kit at the back of a drawer."

"Have you tested it against Miss Welbourne's DNA?"

"That takes a lot longer than you'd think, Janey. But his fingerprints were on it and some blood and hair. The blood group is easy to determine, but not evidence enough.

"Jane," he went on, "wouldn't you think a reasonable person would have gone out late at night, found a block where trash bins were sitting out for pickup in the morning, and put the Dopp kit in one of them?"

"Does he seem to be mentally impaired?"

"Not at all. He even said he'd found out where his mother had her meetings and wanted to talk to her, but she called the police and he went away."

"Where are they now?"

"In separate cells where they can't hear or talk to each other. By law, we can only hold them for twenty-four hours. But the house will be watched by a fleet of officers."

"Can you explain to the rest of my family why you bolted after the first dance?"

"Just generally, without any names."

Two weeks later, Mel told Jane, "They're back in Perth, with all of the documentation, and the brother will be charged with murder. He was handcuffed for the flight to a marshal at the back of the plane and his sister was handcuffed to another marshal at the front. The sister claimed she didn't know what he'd done and was so very sorry he'd killed their mother. Acted as if it was the most horrible thing she'd ever heard. She was a very bad liar. Couldn't even fake tears. She's being charged as an accomplice."

"You did a good job, Mel. And your office will be ready on Friday to move your things in," Jane said.

A week later, Jane watched as the Salvation Army truck levered out the stove and refrigerator from Mel's apartment. Then the smaller items came out, the bread machine still in its box, and the electric meat slicer that from the picture on the box looked as if it could cut through a finger or two like butter. Then the box with the Cuisinart that looked big enough to use on a cruise ship that had to make salsa for a thousand people a day.

There were boxes labeled dishes, silverware, and glassware. Mel had already taken all his clothing and computer parts away to Jane's house.

After he'd returned the key to the apartment, he came back outside, grinning and saluting Jane. "It's done! I'll follow you home."

The office was finished. There was a dark green carpet, walls painted ivory, a cherrywood-finish set of desk, file drawers, and a huge amount of shelving. He had blinds on the windows that Jane had helped him pick out. They even had screens, for a breeze on nice spring and fall days. Jane had feared that the dark carpet and dark shelving would make the room dreary, but the three big windows and doors and cream paint made it cheerful.

When Mel arrived a few minutes after Jane, she said, "Let's go buy that grill for you. I even bought you books about what you can cook on it. I suggest you have Todd and John Nowack put it together for us. They are good at following the instructions."

As they sat outside at the patio table under the umbrella watching the boys lay out all the pieces in order, and reading the instructions, Mel asked, "How are your parents liking their condo?"

"Fine so far. Food is an issue. The kitchen had the essentials. Stove, double ovens, dishwasher, microwave, and fridge. They've bought a kitchen table and chairs.

And dishes, silverware, two tablecloths, pots and pans, a toaster, and stuff like a Cuisinart. They've learned how to make toast and scrambled eggs, but eat out at local restaurants the rest of the time.

"I helped them buy a bed, linens, bedside tables and lamps, as well as a big dresser. But the dining room and living room are empty."

"Not even a television?"

"No. My mother doesn't want one at all and my dad wants a huge plasma screen. My mother's getting stingy about all these purchases."

"They can't be poor."

"They aren't. My dad told me about his pension. It's fabulous. And my mother has one as well as his wife who did years of entertaining. They also have stocks and mutual funds. They're richer than I am."

"The grill is ready," Todd said. "Do you want to learn how to turn it on?"

Mel grinned and got up. "I guess that's a good place to start."

He came back to the table and said, "I think we should invite your folks over tonight for steaks and baked potatoes."

"Don't you think it might be a good idea to try this out first on the three of us before we invite them?"

"Oh, I guess you're right. If I mess it up, only Todd and you will know."

He rummaged through the fridge and found three T-bone steaks. Also three baking potatoes, and an assortment of vegetables. Red peppers, a summer squash, some green beans, an onion, and a cucumber.

He'd already turned on the grill and started cutting the potatoes in long quarters.

"Why are you doing that?" Jane asked.

"Because they'd take a full hour to cook through. Do you have aluminum foil and butter?"

Jane showed him where both of them lived and tucked the vegetables and potatoes neatly on a plate with the steaks. With the recipe book under his left arm, he asked, "How does Todd like his steak done?"

"Well."

"Waste of a good steak." Both he and Jane liked theirs medium-rare.

Everything came out at the same time and was delicious.

"You *are* good at this," Jane said. "My parents have a grill in the middle of their stove. We'll do this again tomorrow and you show my father how to do it."

The day had been hot, but it turned cool by nine and Jane and Mel sat at the patio table, each drinking a half glass of red wine.

When Mel had finished his, he stood and stretched; "It's been a long day. Want to go to bed early?"

"Yes," Jane said with a big smile.